BUCKSKIN, BLOOMERS, *and* ME

Center Point
Large Print

Books are produced in the United States using U.S.-based materials

Books are printed using a revolutionary new process called THINKtech™ that lowers energy usage by 70% and increases overall quality

Books are durable and flexible because of Smyth-sewing

Paper is sourced using environmentally responsible foresting methods and the paper is acid-free

Also by Johnny D. Boggs and available from Center Point Large Print:

The Killing Trail
Return to Red River
Wreaths of Glory
The Raven's Honor
Poison Spring
Taos Lightning
Greasy Grass
MacKinnon
The Fall of Abilene
The Cane Creek Regulators

This Large Print Book carries the Seal of Approval of N.A.V.H.

BUCKSKIN, BLOOMERS, *and* ME

JOHNNY D. BOGGS

CENTER POINT LARGE PRINT
THORNDIKE, MAINE

This Center Point Large Print edition
is published in the year 2019 by arrangement with
Golden West Literary Agency.

December 2019
First Edition

Printed in the United States of America
on permanent paper.
Set in 16-point Times New Roman type.

ISBN: 978-1-64358-439-3

The Library of Congress has cataloged this record
under Library of Congress Control Number: 2019948907

For
the last *Dallas Times Herald*
People's Revolutionary Softball Team, 1991

CHAPTER ONE

The Blues lost the opening and closing games of the season, to say nothing of the ninety-seven other games which they neglected to win. St. Paul took the first and the rival town of Minneapolis took the last. Probably the most wretched season in baseball in Kansas City came to an inglorious close at 4:40 o'clock yesterday afternoon, when a Miller brought in the winning run on a passed ball that did not roll fifteen feet from the plate.

The Kansas City Journal
Kansas City, Missouri
September 20, 1897

He rode into my life on a real fine train just this past summer. "Call me Buckskin," he said, but I'll get to him directly. First, I want to tell how come Buckskin, and a lot of other folks, and me met, including the wretched woman who put me through this ordeal.

Any of you who has had the misfortune to

7

meet the Widow Amy DeFee in person knows I ain't stretching the truth at all when I call her the vilest, repulsivest, meanest, contemptiblist, and poorest excuse for a woman ever to set foot in Kansas, Missouri, and Colorado. And whilst she can handle a .30-30 Winchester better than Annie Oakley, and knows more than most folks about the game of baseball—admittedly, she sure learnt me enough—nobody ever educated her that kidnapping, theft, graft, crooked gambling, horse theft, and especially murder is criminal, and she plumb forgot all them rules of good sportsmanship, honesty, and the fact that it ain't winning that matters most, it's the way you play the game, which is how good folks, good ballists, and us Westerners keep our heads held high— 'cause we play and live the right way. And we don't kill nobody, neither, in blood colder than a hibernating rattlesnake.

But, well, there just ain't no other way to put it but true: The Widow Amy DeFee ain't got nothing in her black heart and blackest of souls but wickedness.

Which is a terrible sentiment to say about your ma.

'Course, she ain't really my ma. Not my birthing ma, I mean. Before I knew the difference between a shine ball and an emery ball, my real ma, Gertrude Grace, died of consumption or cholera or colic or ringworm, depending on how much John Barleycorn Pa had consumed and just who he happened to be relaying the story to on how he become a widower. That's when Pa took to drink worser than he had back when Ma was living. There wasn't no kin left on either side of the family. We wasn't steady church-goers even when Ma was alive, and Ma took care of all my schooling, which weren't much except for them McGuffeys, so it didn't take long before Pa learnt that he needed someone to care for me, else he'd never find time to get roostered while rolling dice down back of the depot.

Therefore, some months after Ma got called to Glory, Pa come across this advertisement in the *Romeo & Juliet Marriage Plan Company Yearbook*:

> White American widow, age 29, weight 105, height 5 feet 4 inches, hazel eyes, brown hair, Baptist, income $700 per annum, good cook, neat, clean, tidy. Will marry if suited.

I read it to Pa, getting plenty of help from the conductor on the Frisco line with them tougher words.

Actually, I had to read all twenty-nine other advertisements, but that's the one that struck Pa's fancy, maybe on account of that $700 figure, but most likely because it was the last one I read before Pa got tired of hearing them words "good housekeeper" and "no flirts will receive attention" and "anxious to meet Western men" and "will answer all correspondence as long as postage is provided."

Too bad Pa never took in one of them shows put on by theatrical troupes when they stopped at the Pleasanton Opera House. Had he seen *Romeo and Juliet*, which I took in a month ago last Thursday, Pa maybe could have figured out that this romance wasn't going to have no happy ending. But what with the Romeo & Juliet Marriage Plan Company being based in Kansas City, Missouri, and us living in Pleasanton and right on the Frisco line, Pa gathered me up and we hopped a freight to Kansas City. We had to do this since Pa, though being employed most of the time by that particular railroad, didn't have no railroad pass and wasn't willing to pay that discounted rate for Frisco workers.

We jumped off after Pa waked me up right before the train pulled into Union Station. That was fun for a seven-year-old, and Pa took to detecting. When he wasn't in his cups, Pa could be right savvy, talk smooth, and fool people into thinking he was a fine citizen and God-fearing daddy. Don't have no idea how he done it, but he got inside the Romeo & Juliet office and found out—to my everlasting regret—that this Widow Amy DeFee lived right there in Kansas

City. Even talked this clerk inside that dumpy little building into sharing the woman's address on Walnut Street. There, Pa persuaded the beer-jerker—the widow lived above a saloon—to tell him that he'd likely find the Widow Amy DeFee over at Exposition Park watching the Blues lose to whoever they was playing on that particular day. That particular day the Blues was playing Minneapolis. They was winning when we got there, but had regressed to their lousy playing by the time Pa found the widow high up on the third-base side of the field.

Even though Exposition Park wasn't filled with spectators on a late September day on account that that year's baseball team was a menace to the sport, it took us a good two-and-a-half innings to track down the woman since that description of her in that matrimonial catalog—a twenty-nine-year-old American Baptist widow all of five-four and a tad over a hundred pounds—wasn't much help, as the widow wasn't none of them things.

Pa found her, though, 'cause he just walked up and down the grandstand, hollering: "Missus Amy DeFee! Missus Amy DeFee! I am seeking the Widow Amy DeFee."

One person stood up and said—"I am Amy DeFee,"—but he wasn't. He was just drunk, which Pa wasn't—not that afternoon. That got a lot of laughs, and even Pa chuckled before he

11

climbed up the steps, then down them again, calling out the widow's name.

Till she rose from her seat, lowered her parasol and bottle of beer, and said: "I am Amy DeFee. Whom am I addressing?"

Just so you know, this ain't all coming from my memories, as I was only seven back then, but from accounts Pa later related to me and the Widow Amy DeFee, not to mention what all them Pinkertons, who is right savvy at this kind of stuff, produced to the judge and assorted peace officers two weeks back.

It must've been the matrimonial catalog that Pa held that give him away, or at least convinced the widow that he wasn't no detective or ordinary copper out to arrest her and get her put in the Jefferson City pen.

Well, ain't no matter now.

Pa, he showed her the catalog, and she saw how he had circled her advertisement over and over again. That impressed her. So they started conversing about whatever folks talk about when they ain't never met or even corresponded by letter like most folks do when seeking potential husbands and budding wives.

I didn't care a whit about Pa or that woman who, I could tell, even young as I was back then, sure didn't look like she was no twenty-nine years old. Getting numbers right sure wasn't among her qualifications as she didn't weigh no

12

one-oh-five, neither, and hadn't in about thirty or forty pounds.

But they must have reached a mutual agreement whilst I ate peanuts and watched the Millers whup that lousy Blues team, 9-to-8, by scoring two runs in the ninth inning.

Pa learnt that the way this here Romeo & Juliet club worked was that if you ever got married, you had to pay the marriage plan seven dollars and fifty cents. That's how the Romeo & Juliet owners earned a living, along with whatever they charged womenfolk to advertise themselves in their yearbook to potential husbands. Talk about heathens and skinflints. My daddy and the widow—she weren't no Baptist—lived in sin to save seven bucks and four bits.

The Widow Amy DeFee was cheap and dishonest and unholy. And, I reckon, you'd have to put Pa in that category, too, but I'd already learnt that much about my daddy long before the widow came into our lives. The Widow Amy DeFee I would get to know right soon. She weren't no widow, I come to figure out. Might've been a bigamist or worse, me later learning about bigamists from Buckskin Compton, who I'll introduce you to once he comes into this story I'm relating, just as I had to do before the judge, the Pinkertons, and the peace officers.

But the Widow Amy DeFee did teach me a

lot about baseball. Took me to games all across eastern Kansas and even into Missouri. Read to me from the sports pages in the newspapers Pa stole from the Frisco trains when he actually went to work, and then the Widow Amy DeFee would tell me what them writers meant. Reckon I learnt more about baseball from her readings than I did by playing the game during those early years. She showed me how to hold a bat and throw the ball. I maybe could have liked her if she hadn't been plumb evil.

Over time, the Widow Amy DeFee told me that she had done as much as she could with me and the great game, but as we weren't rich, I might be able to help out. Being Pa's son, I wasn't no hand around the house, and I was too young to go to work for the Frisco, but in 1903, back when I was only thirteen, she had bought me a bicycle—well, I guess, knowing her, she might have stole it. Anyway, whether the velocipede, which is what Pa always insisted on calling my bicycle, come to our house by honest or dishonest means, that's when I started pedaling from one town to another, picking up quarters and dimes—and after I turned fifteen, sometimes fifty cents or a whole dollar—playing baseball games—which I got to keep for myself.

Till Pa up and died. Got drunk and swallowed his tongue, said the doctor, the sheriff's deputy, and Judge Brett. After that, I had to pay half my baseball earnings to the Widow Amy DeFee, who had suddenly produced a marriage license and an insurance policy which she then showed to Judge Kevin Brett, who wrote a threatening letter to that company in Topeka, warning them that they had better not be planning on stiffing a widow and her young, invalided son—it took me a while to figure out what *invalided* meant and that I wasn't invalided, or no kin to that rotten woman. The judge also told them that he had the honor and privilege to have been riding with General Pleasonton in 'Sixty-Four when the boys in blue turned back the Rebels at Mine Creek and kept Kansas out of Confederate control, and that the Brett name meant something in this state—it didn't, but folks in Topeka ain't real smart—and especially in Linn County 'cause it was the judge who helped found Pleasanton in 'Sixty-Nine and get the first post office here. My pard Buckskin Compton, who I'll tell you about directly as I said before, later pointed out to me that if Judge Kevin Brett was with General Pleasonton during the War of the Rebellion, then how come he didn't get the name spelled right when he got the town founded and the post office established?

You see, Buckskin noticed that the town's name is spelt with an *a-n* in the middle whilst the general used an *o-n*.

But where was I?

Oh, yeah. That occultist Amy DeFee. (Buckskin also told me what *occultist* meant and how to spell it. He's real smart.)

So, let me tell you all about Buckskin Compton and how we become pards as it just ain't good for a body to spend all this time penning and then scratching out words and ripping up whole pages and starting over again, especially whilst writing a lot about a mean, evil occultist, which is, Buckskin Compton tells me, like a witch or evil sorceress. Or as Louis Friedman, who I'll also get to later, described the Widow Amy DeFee: "Jezebel, the Witch of Endor, and Lizzie Borden stuffed inside one corset."

See, Pa'd been dead two months, it being 1906, and I'd been velocipeding, as my Pa would have said, from town to town practically every available day since the burying, earning my keep, and helping keep the Widow Amy DeFee in elderberry wine with my earnings playing baseball for mostly town-ball teams in Kansas and just over the border in Missouri.

So in early May, I took bat and glove and pedaled close to ten miles mostly west but a little south to Mound City, which is the county seat even though Pleasanton's got more people, not to mention the Frisco line, but is closer to Missouri. Likely Mound City, which does have the Missouri Pacific, got the county seat job because you never want the law and all that

16

important stuff to be too close to bushwhackers and Missouri ruffians.

On this particular day, I was playing shortstop, though I preferred second base, for Mound City, which was battling the team from Garnett over and up in Anderson County. We beat them pretty good because there ain't nothing much good that ever comes out of Anderson County, and after Rufus Durant, manager and third baseman of the Mound City team, paid me my seventy-five cents, he asked: "What are you doing the Nineteenth?"

I say: "You need me for a game?"

He says: "Not just any game. We're playing the National Bloomer Girls."

I say: "The what?"

Which made him take a step back and cock his head and give me a look that means surely I can't be that ignorant.

But I can.

"Surely you've heard of the Bloomer Girls," he told me.

"No, sir, I surely ain't," I tell him.

He grinned, shook his head, and said: "Well, they're a traveling team of ballists in bloomers. Females, you see. There are teams of Bloomers all across the nation these days. Cleveland. Indianapolis. New York City. This particular team hails from Kansas City. Or is it Boston? Anyway, they'll be here on the Nineteenth. I'd sure love to

17

have you, because the last thing I want to do is lose to petticoats."

"I thought they was Bloomers."

He straightened, studied me for what seemed like a long time, and finally asked again if I was available to play baseball on that Saturday.

Well, I was about to tell Rufus Durant that I really don't want to play a bunch of girls, and it don't matter if they're wearing bloomers or petticoats, but May 19th happens to be a Saturday and nobody else has asked me or the Widow Amy DeFee if I can play for them on that particular day, when Rufus Durant says something that sure snatched my attention.

"I'll pay you a dollar and a half."

I'm reaching for the handlebars to my bicycle, but I look at him to make sure he ain't joshing.

"And," Rufus Durant says, "I'll tell your step-mother that I'm paying you seventy-five cents."

Right quick I learnt that I can be as dishonest as the Widow Amy DeFee.

"I'll see you Saturday. What time?"

CHAPTER TWO

Mound City, Kan., May 19—For the first time in the history of the office of probate judge of Linn county a young woman secured her own license to marry. Miss Maude Fidelia Lacy, of Kansas City, Mo., aged 18, got a license for herself to wed Ernest Earl Foster of Hannibal, Mo., aged 22. After she had left the probate judge's office Foster met her, and Rev. J.M. Iliff united them in marriage. Miss Lacy plays second base on the National Bloomer Girls' baseball team.

Parsons Daily Eclipse
Parsons, Kansas
Saturday, May 19, 1906

So that Saturday, the 19th, I pedaled hard, carrying my good bat and my only glove, and got to Mound City pretty early, expecting to find the pasture where the Mound City Nine played their games, but, boy howdy, I thought my mind somehow got addled and that I'd rid to the wrong town because that pasture didn't look like no pasture at all.

I mean to tell you there was grandstand set up, and canvas fences—six foot high, mind you—around the outfield, and I could smell peanuts and parched corn, and there was horses and mules and even more bicycles and farm wagons and phaetons, some with canopies and some without, a couple of road carts, and even an omnibus that had hauled what seemed the whole population of Mapleton from down south a ways. Plus a line of folks at the gate.

Which is where some idiot told me I had to pay him twenty-five cents to get in, but I let him know that I was a ballist—even showed him my bat and glove—and was playing for Mound City. He, a dark-skinned fellow with shifty eyes and a crooked nose, give me a look that made me think he was calling me a liar and a cheat, which got my ears to burning. But then here come Mr. Durant, and he told that fellow that I was the starting second baseman and not to give me or him no guff.

The lady behind me patted my shoulder and said—"Knock the stuffing out of 'em harlots,"—and I didn't know what to say to that but didn't have to on account that Mr. Durant was pulling me through the throng and under the fence that separated the paying folk from the playing folk. There he give me a cap and a jersey, one of them bib-front jerseys, with a big blue **M** for Mound on the bib but no **C** for City, and said I'd have to play in my Blue Buckles, but that didn't matter much on account that all the Mound City ballists wore different kinds of pants—duck trousers, patched woolens, and a couple even had overalls like mine. Anyway, Mr. Durant thanked me for coming, and started saying a few things, but by that point, having rode a bicycle nigh ten miles, I weren't listening to him much but just wishing he might offer me a drink of water. But then I figured it likely wasn't water he was drinking from his flask, so I started looking across the field and watching them Bloomer girls practice.

Didn't look like harlots, iffen you was to ask me. Fact is, they looked more like a baseball team than us Mound City contingent. (Buckskin Compton told me to use the word *contingent* and how it's spelt.)

They wore dark blue uniforms, complete with belts, and those baggy pants that give them their name. Their stockings was blue, too, but with a white stripe just before the bloomers stopped right at their knees. Their hats was blue wool flannel with white trim—what we ballists call an eight-panel cap since the white trim divides the blue wool into eight panels—with a small, rounded brim. They had collared shirts, with pearl button fronts—not fancy bibs like us Mound City boys—and that reminded me that I needed to put on my own shirt but didn't want to do it in front of a bunch of ladies because I got manners. Most of them Bloomers wore under-sleeves on account it was sort of chilly if you hadn't pedaled a bicycle ten miles.

Them gals looked sorta pretty, except for two of them who was plug-ugly, but not as ugly as their manager. He had a big gut, and wore a flat-crowned, flat-brimmed straw hat with a big black band around the crown, and a white shirt with a narrow tie, plaid pants, and scuffed Wellingtons. He smoked a cigar while twisting the ends of his mustache, and he was spitting out words that you wasn't supposed to say to ladies or anywhere in Kansas unless you was in Dodge City before it got religion.

Well, Mr. Durant wasn't a whole lot better.

"Look at 'em," Mr. Durant told me once he realized I wasn't paying him much mind. After a whole lot of blasphemy, he spit on a cow pie—this still being a pasture—and said: "In my day, you never even saw a woman playing one-eyed cat or wicket. It was bad enough when they started thinking they could play croquet or go out boating. Now they think they can do anything. Golf. Ride bicycles. It's a disgrace. Shames our nation. Might even be the beginning of the end of the world. The 'New Woman.' Balderdash!" Only he used another word that wasn't balderdash.

I opened my mouth and started to ask him why

he was playing them ladies if that's the way he felt, but then I figured that wouldn't be a smart thing to say iffen I wanted my buck fifty, which I did, especially since the Widow Amy DeFee didn't know how much I was truly getting paid for this here game. Besides, it wasn't like I had a whole lot of time to say something because he kept right on with his blaspheming and spitting and complaining.

"Turning baseball into a burlesque. How far will the government let our national pastime fall in disgrace?"

The Mound City hurler, a lanky fireman for the Missouri Pacific, walked up and slapped Mr. Durant on the shoulder, and said: "As far as you'll let 'em for twenty percent of the gate, boss."

Mr. Durant spit. "Twenty-five percent, bucko." He turned and bellowed where in the blazes—but it weren't blazes that he said—was that Lutheran minister who had agreed to umpire the game. Then he looked at me and told me to hurry up and get my shirt on. That got my face flushing, but I figured, it being on the cool side for this time of year, I'd just pull it over my three-for-a-dollar shirt no matter how warm I'd gotten pedaling ten miles.

After that, the right fielder, who was smoking a corncob pipe, asked if I wanted to toss the ball with him, which I did, and things went on like that, me throwing the ball with a pipe-smoker and Mr. Durant cussing the Bloomers when he wasn't taking a nip from his flask. So folks filled them grandstand, eating food and drinking lemonade till that bald-headed, bespectacled Lutheran finally showed up to umpire, and we prayed. Then we tossed the ball some more, or swung our bats, and got ready to play the National Bloomer Girls.

When Mound City come to bat in the first inning, I led off, 'cause I run pretty fast, and that's why I played second base mostly. I took my bat up to the plate, and nodded at the catcher, and said howdy to the Lutheran ump, and stepped up and give the pitcher the meanest glare I could in order to intimidate her on account Mr. Durant told me to do that. Normally, I wouldn't've because even though my pa had his faults, he had always taught me to be kind to ladies, puppy dogs, and veterans of the War of the Rebellion as long as they'd worn the blue. This in spite of the fact that his parents hadn't gotten off the boat from Wales until 1867!

The Bloomer hurler, though, didn't look or act scared at all, and she sent a fastball that sounded like a cannon when it popped into the catcher's big mitt. Then I could hear Mr. Durant hollering from his bench.

"I remember the time when nobody . . . and I mean not one man . . . ever wore a mitt at all, especially not one the size of a pillow . . . anywhere on the gosh-darned field." 'Course, he didn't say gosh-darned.

The catcher, well, she didn't say nothing, just throwed the ball right back, hard, to the lady pitcher, whilst I was blinking, thinking to myself: *I don't think I saw that ball once it left that southpaw's hand.*

So I looked back at the Lutheran, and he stared at me, and I asked him: "Was that a strike, Preacher?" Because for a Lutheran and an umpire, he wasn't a real loud talker.

Right then I felt the wind rush past my kneecap and saw dust pop in the catcher's mitt, and that catcher tossed the ball up out of her mitt, snatched the ball with her right hand, and fired it back to that hard-throwing, left-handed Bloomer girl.

Well, I looked back at the pitcher, then down at the catcher, and then back at the umpire, and the Lutheran said: "Yes, lad, the lady's first throw was across the plate right about at your belt buckle. Just the same as that one. And . . ."

The grimace on his lips and the fear in his eyes told me that that sneaky Bloomer girl was sending another baseball toward the plate, whilst my back was to her. I turned around and started to bring my bat up, but, almost too late, I saw that that ball wasn't coming belt-high across the plate but right toward my noggin.

That's when I let out a dirty word while leaping backward, dropping my big bat, and falling on my hindquarters. Everybody in them fancy grandstand and even those skinflints who was sitting on their horses on the other side of the canvas fence the Bloomers had set up in the pasture, laughed, hooted, and mocked me. Along the bench of the home team, my teammates sniggered, too.

"That," the Lutheran said, "was not a strike, and I fear I must call it a ball."

"What's the matter?" said the catcher, whose voice was raspy. "Didn't like that pitch?" She laughed as she rose, knees popping, threw the ball back, though softer this time.

My ears started burning. Standing over me was the third basewoman, smiling as she stuck her glove under her armpit and reached down, extending her throwing hand to help me up.

"He ain't hurt, Dolly," the catcher told her.

Now, what with catchers wearing big masks by 1906—Mr. Durant would go off about that, too, when he was in his cups, which he usually was, but maybe not as often as my late pa—I couldn't see much about the catcher other than she had big hands for a girl and was dark-haired and flat-chested. Same as Dolly Madison—I didn't know nothing about the Dolly Madison of our nation's history till Buckskin Compton told me all about her—the third basewoman whose grip

26

felt like my pa's when he was swinging a sixteen-pound sledge-hammer steadily rather than lifting a pint.

I got a right good look at Dolly Madison, who had piercing blue eyes and full lips and blonde hair all curly and full. She was taller than me and had broad shoulders to boot.

"That's Lady Waddell's way of introducing herself," said the third basewoman in a friendly kind of way, and then introduced herself and tipped her curly blonde head over at the catcher. "And she's Nellie McConnell."

I nodded at them both, but not that dastardly little witch of a pitcher, and let Nellie settle back behind the plate and Dolly trot back to third base as I dusted off my heinie, and checked my bat to make sure it hadn't been damaged. Once I was back in my stance, I set my jaw and tried not to listen to them folks in the grandstand who was yelling that I was a bum and ought to go back to Pleasanton or someplace hotter and way below sea level.

Lady Waddell threw a ball, but my eyesight told me that it was spinning away, and it spun right into the dirt a good foot off the plate. The catcher had to leap over and snag the ball, not that it would've done any harm as that made the count only two strikes and two balls and there wasn't nobody on base because I was the first batter in this ball game.

All right, I told myself as I gripped the bat's handle firmly and ground my teeth as I saw the ball coming again. I let it travel some before I stepped into that pitch, swung the bat, felt the stinging in my hands, and watched that ball carry over the right fielder's head, and that told me something 'cause I never ever hardly get a ball to that side of the field, even against a southpaw. I took off running, and I kept right on running, till I went into a slide and come up in the dust at third base with a triple that had them Mound City folks hollering and screaming and jumping up and down and saying that I was the best player that Mound City had ever seen since King Kelly. But I figured none of them had actually seen King Kelly play as I'd never heard that he'd been to Mound City and he'd been dead for around ten years.

Dolly Madison grinned at me and threw the ball back to the pitcher and told me: "Not many ballists I know can hit that pitch off Lady Waddell. How long have you been playing baseball?"

We chatted some, her being real friendly and me not knowing hardly a soul on my own team, which wasn't my own team as I was just a traveling velocipedist, who played for whoever was paying me. It struck me then that wouldn't it be nice iffen I could play for just one team.

Turned out to be a pretty good baseball contest.

I would've been satisfied with just that triple, but I also singled, and stole second base—actually I was out, but the umpire didn't call it that way. The second basewoman swore a mite but let it go. When I come up to bat for the last time in the eighth inning, the catcher said that I knew I was out (which was true), that she knew I was out, that everyone in the grandstand and even them misers watching the game from beyond the outfield fence knew, that God knew, and that everybody knew I was out except for the blind Lutheran umpire.

The Lutheran said meekly: "From my view and my humble opinion, he got under the tag, ma'am."

I walked on seven pitches but didn't try stealing no bases or make it to third to chat some more with Dolly Madison because I didn't get a chance as Al Iverson grounded weakly into a double play, and that ended our last at-bat 'cause we didn't need to bat in the ninth inning on account that we was the home team after the coin flip. We won the game 7-to-4. Besides, the Bloomer girls had to catch the Missouri Pacific so they wanted to get everything packed up, including the canvas fences and the bleachers which I learnt they carried with them to all their contests.

Well, I got my money from Mr. Durant, and after I'd shaken hands with my teammates and them Bloomer girls, I was out of the pasture and heading to my bicycle when that tobacco-chewing manager of them girls came up to me and holds out his hand and introduces hisself as Ed Norris.

"Where you from?" he asked me after I told him my name. I pointed and started to say Pleasanton, but then I got suspicious and thought that maybe if he found out that I wasn't from Mound City, he might protest that we was cheating him and then the Lutheran might declare a forfeit and Mr. Durant might ask for his money back that he had paid me. Instead, I just bobbed my head toward the northeast and said—"Over yonder a ways,"—which wasn't no lie. I sure hoped he didn't want to invite hisself to supper, but I didn't figure he would on account that they was so jo-fired on catching that train.

I got to thinking as I glanced back toward the Mound City baseball field that was quickly returning to resembling the pasture it was, that this crew that worked with the Bloomer Girls was sure skilled in taking down them grandstand and canvas fences in no time at all.

"You play good second base, run well, can hit," Mr. Ed Norris said, which made me straighten up and feel pretty good till he went right on: "And you're fair-skinned, aren't shaving yet, and are soft-spoken."

I didn't know what to say to that, so I just stood there with my mouth drawing flies.

"How old are you?" he asked, quickly adding: "Not that it matters."

"Sixteen," I said.

He chewed on a pencil, looked this way and that, saying: "I suppose we'd have to get your parents' permission."

I didn't say nothing 'cause I didn't know what he was talking about, but I figured it out a moment later

"Listen, Maude Lacy has been my regular second bagger, but . . ."—he paused to spit tobacco juice and do a mite of soft cussing— "the thing is she up and got married. Married some fool from Hannibal, and nothing good has come out of Hannibal since Mark Twain left. Well, the rules are only unwed women can play for the National Bloomer Girls, and they're already in a hurry to have a baby . . . Maude and that reprobate Ernest Earl Foster, I mean . . . so they've gone back to Missouri. I wish her well, but this Foster fellow can get lost in a cave like Injun Joe for all I care."

I didn't know what the Sam Hill he was talking about till Buckskin Compton bought a copy of *The Adventures of Tom Sawyer* wrote by that fellow Twain whose name wasn't Twain at all but Samuel Clemens, and then made me read it on the train. Buckskin read part of the book to me on account that my slow reading or bad pronouncing or asking him what some word meant or how it was to be said aloud annoyed him at times.

"Listen," Mr. Ed Norris said to me, "how would you like to play second base for us?"

I just snorted, because I wasn't going to laugh at being played for a fool. I went right to work lashing my big bat underneath the handlebars to my bicycle as that was the easiest way for me to carry it after I'd stuffed my glove into the pack I wore on my back that also carried my tool bag, my lunch pail, a can of lubricating oil, my Burlington Cyclist Cape in case it happened to rain, and a Demon Lamp from the Sears, Roebuck & Co., Incorporated, in case it got dark before I could make it home, which sometimes it did and might that day if I kept letting this pot-bellied manager keep on with his flapdoodle.

"I'm serious," he told me. "I need a second baseman in a hurry. For the rest of our season. I hear you can pitch some, too."

Now the hairs started standing up on the back of my neck as I squatted there. I looked up at him above the handlebars to tell him: "Mister, I ain't no girl."

"Neither am I."

That's when I turned and saw the third base-woman Dolly Madison, still in her Bloomer Girl uniform, but taking off her—I mean *his*—wig.

Well, I gawked, swallowed, coughed, and quickly turned back around. But by now all the Mound City folks had gone back to their homes and even that omnibus was out of sight with its passel of folks headed back to Mapleton, so there wasn't nobody around the pasture except the Bloomer Girls and all them workers getting everything packed up to take to the Missouri Pacific depot.

"Bill Compton's the name," the third base-woman . . . base-*man* . . . said as he stepped up, holding out his hand. "Call me Buckskin."

She . . . *he* . . . needed a shave. I could see that now. But I took his hand.

Buckskin turned back to Mr. Norris and said: "You got any Big Chunk?"

"You know I only chew Sure Pop," Ed Norris fired back.

"One of these days you'll get wise," said Bill "Buckskin" Compton, alias Dolly Madison. "But I suppose it'll have to do."

Now that I was paying attention, when he held out his hand, I saw that it was not only too big to belong on a female of her . . . *his* . . . size, but that there were hairs on its knuckles.

After Buckskin got a plug from Mr. Norris, he bit off a chaw, and stuffed the rest of the tobacco in his trousers pocket. "I'll pay you back in Fort Scott," he told Mr. Norris before looking at me. When he had that tobacco softened enough by his teeth, he asked: "You joining us?"

Well, I had no inkling of going around dressed up like a woman and making a fool out of myself

33

all across Kansas, and I took to studying them other Bloomer Girls as they loaded their stuff into a wagon. I shook my head and must've had the face of some Lutheran who thought them Bloomer Girls was defrauding the good people of Kansas by pretending they was girls.

"Most of them are girls," Buckskin said.

"But dames can't pitch or catch worth a fip," Mr. Norris said, though he didn't use the word *fip*. "So, yeah, we bring in a few toppers."

"Toppers?" I asked.

Buckskin held up his wig. "Ringers," he explained, and I knew what a ringer was, me being a ringer on account teams from all over eastern Kansas paid me to come play for them.

"Speaking of wigs," Mr. Norris said, "you best put yours back on before Ruth sees you."

Buckskin rolled his eyes but did as he was told. I turned to see if I could find this Ruth. She played first base, and she had to be a girl, as she played that position wearing a catcher's mitt, but she played it real good. Plus, she was right pretty. By golly, I sure was glad *she* wasn't no man.

But using toppers or ringers, well, that explained why Lady Waddell throwed so hard and had one nasty curveball, and was more likely a brother than a sister to Rube Waddell, the great southpaw who'd won something like twenty-five or more games for the Philadelphia Athletics last season.

"And the catcher?" I asked, because it suddenly struck me just how stupid I was not to figure him out as a scalawag of a scoundrel and a he instead of a she.

Buckskin Compton told me: "When you're on the train, you can call Nellie McConnell Nelse. He's a good Irish lass." That last sentence Buckskin said in a humorous Irish accent.

Only I wasn't laughing.

"I can work out a payment arrangement with your folks," Mr. Norris said, but by that time I was pulling my pack up over my shoulders and getting ready to pedal those ten miles home before it got dark.

Suddenly Mr. Norris blurted out what he would pay me, and if I'd taken up the habit of chewing tobacco I would've likely swallowed juice and chaw and gotten sicker than a dog right then and there.

I shouted: "A week?"

Which almost caused Buckskin to swallow his tobacco as he got to laughing so hard.

Mr. Ed Norris chuckled a mite, too, and corrected me. "A game."

CHAPTER THREE

It developed at the ball game yesterday, between the Fort Scott Athletics and the National Bloomer "Girls" that the girls were men of the Lilliputian type and that they wore wigs to conceal their identity. However, there were two women on the team, the second baseman and the center fielder, neither of which got their hands on the ball at all. The fact is, they were afraid of the ball and when it came near them, they would get out of the way of it. There were three other girls that did not appear in the field at all. They played the bench. It was a novel game to hoodwink the people and it worked to perfection.

The Fort Scott Tribune and Monitor
Fort Scott, Kansas
May 21, 1906

Sometimes, you don't realize how lucky you are. What I'm saying is that all my life I wanted a horse to ride, and would've settled for a pony or even a mule. But, living in town, or right next to town, and what with my pa working for a railroad when he actually worked, I always got lectured that I didn't need no horse. Then the Widow Amy DeFee give me this bicycle, which wasn't brand new, I don't think, but I had seen one just like it in the Montgomery Ward & Co.'s Catalog that cost sixty-five dollars, which was more than most folks paid for horses in these parts. I also always wanted a dog. Never get one, though.

But here's what I mean when I say how lucky I was by not getting what I'd dreamt of getting.

Had I been riding a horse, the Widow Amy DeFee and Judge Kevin Brett would have heard me trotting up to our house. Had I owned a puppy dog, it would have barked as I pedaled up. Or had I even dickered around about the money and what all I was to be doing for the National Bloomer Girls baseball team, I likely would have had to light up my lamp and them two might have seen the light shining in the dark and knew I was almost home. Turns out, it was just getting dark as I pedaled up to the house out on the edge of town, and bicycling is a quiet way to travel.

Still, I wanted to shout and let them hear the news that I was about to become a professional baseball player—even if I was going to be playing on a girls team that had three men wearing wigs and bloomers already.

But, first, let me tell you about the deal I'd struck up with Mr. Norris.

"I ain't gonna wear no wig," I told him.

"Your hair's long and curly enough as it is," he assured me. "And you're fair-skinned. Nice complexion for a Kansas farm boy." I didn't let him know that I wasn't raised on no farm but come from a town—a city, by grab—so I just glared.

My face got red again when Nelson "Nellie" McConnell come up and said: "I thought he was a lovely little lass when he first come to bat." He talked Irish, but he wasn't faking it like Buckskin had done earlier. "Says to myself, I say . . . 'Why the good people of Mound City wanted to give us a chance, playing a girl against an all-girls team.' Ain't that a bloody laugh. You got any chawing tobaccy, Ed?"

"Criminy," Ed Norris said, and found another plug in his pocket, which he tossed to Nelson McConnell. Then the manager looked at me. "Can you catch?"

"I can play anywhere you put me," I let him know. And I would—for what he was going to pay me.

"Well, go get your folks. We can get this done in a hurry. Have to."

A train whistle screeched, and then Ed Norris blowed his top.

"There's no time now," he said, and strung together just about every dirty word I'd ever heard and even a couple I'd never heard even whispered on a dare on any baseball diamond. "Can you get to Fort Scott for tomorrow's game? Starts at two-thirty."

"Tomorrow's Sunday," I reminded him.

"Yeah. Baseball's church to some of us. Can you get there?"

He didn't wait for me to answer. "Listen, if you can't get there by then, fine. I can play Ruth again. She gets tired of selling programs anyway, and her ma would appreciate it."

"She's not that bad of a player," Buckskin said, which made Nelson McConnell snort and spit juice between Buckskin's baseball shoes.

"Thinks you," McConnell said.

"Shut up," Mr. Norris said. "If you can't get to Fort Scott on time, our next game's Monday in Galesburg. If you aren't there by Monday, I'll figure you've decided you'd rather slop hogs and milk cows and pick taters than make a fortune with our higgledy-piggledy."

He shook my hand, as did Buckskin, and the three walked toward the bus of lady ballists. I stared at them, wondering which other ones had flim-flammed me into thinking they was actual girls. Then I settled into the saddle on my Hawthorne bicycle and started pedaling for home, thinking along the way about how I might higgledy-piggledy the Widow Amy DeFee into thinking that I wasn't going to be making nowhere near the kind of money I'd actually been promised.

Pretty much out of breath, I reached our shack, and leaned my bicycle against the fence, which could barely hold it up, the fence being in mighty poor condition. I took out the money the Widow Amy DeFee expected me to pay her, hoping she hadn't learnt how much money I had been paid, and moved toward the front door. I'd seen the judge's buggy, and could tell from the horse's panting and the lather on its neck that the judge had just got there and that he had drove real hard. He lived on the other side of town, in the fine section, but Pleasanton ain't that big of a burg, so the judge had drove his rig fast and worn out his horse something awful.

I just about got to the porch when the Widow Amy DeFee's voice brought me to a dead stop.

"A will? What do you mean he left a will?"

"Land sakes, Amy, quiet down," Judge Brett told her. "A clerk in probate found it. I didn't know. You didn't know. Nobody knew."

"And nobody has to know." The Widow Amy DeFee said some other things that weren't very lady-like.

The judge whispered something.

I started again for the porch, but then whatever the judge had told her must have set off the Widow Amy DeFee's fuse on account she shrieked again. "A newspaper. You let a newspaper reporter see the will?" She give the judge an earful.

"What could I do?" he pleaded.

"He's leaving everything . . . to . . . that . . . boy?"

"It's not like he had much."

"He would have had less, if we hadn't forged that life insurance policy," said the Widow Amy DeFee, followed by cursing and stomping. "Now that half-wit who's good for nothing except baseball gets my fortune."

"Please settle down, Amy," the judge pleaded.

I felt cold, on account that once the sun had gone down, I'd sweated an awful lot pedaling my way back home as fast as I could. Dumb and ignorant as I was, my legs again started taking me to the porch, and likely would've done just that had I not heard the next words of the Widow Amy DeFee.

"You have to kill him."

The judge let out a gasp, which was a good thing because I done that exact same thing.

"My word . . . he's a boy," the judge cautioned.

I wasn't walking no more, but sweating, feeling sick, and wanting to vomit.

"You're the one who bungled this . . . ," she said.

"It's not my fault."

"You have to kill him."

"I'll do no such thing."

"You killed *him*."

Right then I felt like I'd misplayed a line drive and the ball had caught me right under the sternum 'cause now I knew that my wicked stepmother not only wanted to murder me, but that she and Judge Brett had murdered my daddy, which hurt most of all, because Pa hadn't gotten drunk and swallowed his tongue like the sheriff's deputy and the doctor and all the newspapers and gossips and friends and railroad workers had said.

It's a hard thing to take in, especially after being happy about playing a good baseball game and beating a team of women—yes, and a few men—and then getting an offer that a kid like me only ever dreamt of getting. And in spite of riding ten miles back and forth that day across southeastern Kansas and not having had much to eat the whole day after a measly breakfast of corn mush and buttermilk, I was so excited at how my life was turning out.

But as I listened to what they was saying, I knew that if I didn't get out of this town, my life was gonna turn out dead.

"They can hang you for one murder, Kevin," the Widow Amy DeFee told the judge. "Or they can hang you for two. Or you and me can be rich and get out of this wretched West."

Right then I started wishing for things other than a pony or a puppy dog. I wished we had neighbors. I wished it wasn't Saturday night and that the sheriff wasn't over at that house that nobody ever talked about unless they was working for the railroad. But then I thought that since the sheriff's deputy had said my daddy had gotten drunk and swallowed his tongue that maybe he was part of this crime, too, 'cause the Widow Amy DeFee knew how to lure good men astray. I couldn't go to the law, anyway, because who would believe a sixteen-year-old kid over a twice-widowed woman and a judge who thought he was mighty important in this neck of the prairie?

Fort Scott.

That's what I thought. Fort Scott. That was my only chance. Mr. Norris said I'd be called Lucy Totton and not nothing else iffen I took to playing for the National Bloomer Girls, so none of my friends—not that I had any—would ever know or figure out that I was playing as a woman on a Bloomers baseball team. He told me that no one could know unless my folks told them. There was a *clause*—that's what Mr. Norris called it—in the contract that said nobody was to know that there was men playing, and that iffen they let that fact slip out, they were in violation of the contract which could be torn up. The violators would even have to pay back all the money they'd been paid by the Bloomer Girls.

It was twenty-five miles to Fort Scott. Almost a straight line south. Good roads, a whole lot better than the one to Mound City. All I had to do was walk back to the fence and get on my Hawthorne. And that's what I was doing when I knew I was found out.

"It's the kid! It's your chance to kill him!" I heard the widow shout.

"Lord have mercy," the judge said. "What if he heard what you said?"

"What I said? You'll swing before they spring a trap door on me, you idiot. Shoot him. Don't let him get away, you ignorant . . ."

I heard the door open, but I didn't listen that closely after that because the gunshot reminded me of that ball Lady Waddell smashed in the fourth inning that plowed into the canvas fence in center field earlier that day. But the bullet that whistled past my head was a whole lot scarier than the fastball the southpaw hurler had thrown at me in the first inning.

"Give me that carbine," the Widow Amy DeFee snapped at the judge, which got me pedaling real hard as I leaned low because I knew how well she could shoot a Winchester.

But there weren't no more gunshots, and I didn't hear the hammer go *click* on that .30-30, but I did hear the Widow Amy DeFee scream: "Why isn't this thing loaded?"

Likely I would be dead and you wouldn't

be reading this narrative, and the judge, jury, lawmen, and newspaper reporters would never have heard my testimony, neither, if that gun had been loaded.

I leaned to my right, held out my leg, felt the sand kicking underneath my shoe, straightened the Hawthorne, and just kept pedaling as hard as I could. Keep right along the road that would take me to Fort Scott. And at the rate I was working them pedals, I figured I might even beat the Missouri Pacific train that was taking the National Bloomer Girls baseball team there, too.

CHAPTER FOUR

The Kansas City National Bloomer Girls ball team was billed to play the local team on the Thayer diamond on Tuesday. The game was timed to begin at 3 o'clock, and the players were ready, a large crowd was in town in anticipation of the event, when just at the time for the game, it began to rain and the game had to be abandoned. But the Bloomer girls say they will play the Thayer team at some future date. . . . There are only four or five girls on the team, the rest being young boys.

The Chanute Tribune
Chanute, Kansas
May 25, 1906

I got to Fort Scott in time for the game. Well, no, I arrived long before the game even started. Pedaling so hard to avoid getting murdered got me there before daybreak, and I hid in a barn at a dairy farm, fearing the Widow Amy DeFee or that murdering, lying no-account judge was tracking me down.

Later, it come to me that maybe they weren't yet following me. After all, the judge had run his horse real hard in that buggy to bring bad news to the widow, so that horse wouldn't be good for more than a mile or two, and it being dark, they wouldn't have no inkling where I'd run off to. I prayed they might think I'd find me a sheriff or marshal or Pinkerton man and that being as they wouldn't want to get hanged by the neck till they was dead, they would flee Kansas and disappear somewhere down in Cuba or South America.

Fort Scott used to be a right thriving town, but then the Army had figured there wasn't nothing worth protecting no more, so it pulled all them soldier boys out ages ago. 'Course, some of the soldiering buildings is still standing. So, as I said, I hid at a dairy farm. Once it got around dawn, I knew the farmer would be out to check on his cows on account that farmers get up earlier than ballists.

Fort Scott was still fair-sized, with railroads and brick buildings and some pretty homes. I just kept my eyes open for anybody who resembled the widow or that rotten judge. When I finally determined that them killers weren't around, I went looking for Mr. Norris and the Bloomers. My Hawthorne would be a dead giveaway, I thought, and regretted using the word *dead* in my thinking, so I affixed—that's another word from Buckskin—my bicycle to a hitching rail at the corner of Crawford and Tenth with my chain and lock. I took my bag and my bat with me.

As there was still plenty of hotels in Fort Scott, I walked back and forth on the boardwalks, waiting to see some ballist or Bloomer I might recognize. Nobody paid attention to me 'cause the businessmen and farmers was all busy talking about important matters like what rates was C.C. Nelson & Co. charging, and how bad had Mrs. Beatty's catarrh got, and was the ManZan Pile Cure as good as Mr. Konantz said it was. I stopped out front of the Lockwood House, not because I thought the Bloomers might be lodged in that place, but on account of the smells that came out of the dining hall. It smelt like bacon, and it struck me that I hadn't eaten nothing since breakfast yesterday, unless you counted some peanuts I crunched on during the ball game. Pains in my stomach stabbed me so bad I had to hurry away.

That's what I was doing when I ran right smack into a gent in a nice suit as he was coming out of Cottrell's Bookstore. Didn't knock him over or even make him lose the books he was carrying. He turned and stared, first at me, then at the big bat I had in my left hand. I wasn't threatening him, nor would I unless I learnt that he had been hired by the judge or widow to kill me. He looked at my face and pushed back his bowler.

"You're . . . ," he began.

"You're Dolly Madison," I said, figuring out who he was first even though it took me a while to recognize him as he wasn't wearing no bloomers nor no blonde wig.

"Buckskin," he corrected. With a grin, he stuffed the books underneath his left armpit and held out his right hand. "Don't tell me your folks broke down and agreed to let you take Ed's offer."

"My pa's dead," I told him, and wished I hadn't because it made the smile vanish off Buckskin Compton's face.

"I'm sorry to hear that," he said.

"Ma's dead, too." I think that was the first time I really understood that I didn't have no parents no more. I wasn't lying.

"That's rough," he said to me.

Well, we stood on the boardwalk, making folks walk around us, because I learnt that when you say something like that, just blurt out rotten news, it pretty much stops a conversation.

But another fellow come up behind Buckskin and changed everything.

"Good morning, I'm Sheriff J.C. Commons."

Now, my first inclination—that's another four-bit word Buckskin taught me, and from here on in you can figure that just about any big word I use come from him—was to tell the sheriff that my ma, though she weren't really my birthing ma, and a judge but not a judge in Bourbon County, which is where I was, were out to murder me. I wasn't sure if judges' duties was restricted to towns or counties like sheriffs or if they could work statewide being as we was still in Kansas. But I didn't get no chance to figure it out on account that Buckskin Compton did the strangest thing. He reached inside his fancy coat and spun on a heel like he was pivoting to try to turn a double play.

But the tall gent beamed like Pa used to after he had a few nips and them hot dice started rolling the dots he wanted, and he announced: "Or I will be sheriff . . . if I can count on your vote."

Buckskin stopped his pivot, but his hand stayed inside his coat, as the tall fellow continued.

"With your support, we can get Roodhouse out of office and bring peace and respectability back to Bourbon County. I've announced my candidacy on the Democratic ticket, but of course that is subject to the will and decision of the Democratic Convention." He had a stack of papers clipped to a board in his left hand. "Might I have your support?"

Buckskin slowly pulled his hand from underneath his coat, wiped it on his trousers leg, and said: "I'm sorry, sir, but I'm just passing through."

"Oh." Mr. Commons looked crestfallen—that's a word I picked up from one of them books Buckskin bought at Cottrell's. And Mr. Commons stepped up to me and said: "And how about you, young man?"

"Y'all got a sheriff named Roadhouse?" I said.

"*Rood*-house," he corrected, but kept right on grinning as he added, "but that might be something I can use in my campaign against that scoundrel." He saw my baseball bat. "Are you twenty-one?"

"He's with me," Buckskin said. "We came to see the Bloomer Girls play your Athletics this afternoon."

"Oh." The candidate looked back at Buckskin, shook his hand once more, and said: "Well, you sha'n't find a better team than ours, sir. We have a reputation of playing like gentlemen. Why, a merchant in Pittsburg said that our team, because of the nature of our players, is the only one in the league that he would dare keep at his hotel. Our team is filled with gentlemen."

"Ours isn't." Buckskin nodded at the gent, whose face looked kind of numb, and told me we best grab some breakfast.

As we walked away, the man who wanted to be sheriff recovered and said that we should try Carey's Pastry Kitchen. Which we did, and when

I was about to tell Buckskin that I didn't have money to buy even coffee, I recollected that I still had the dollar and fifty cents that I'd been paid by Mr. Durant in Mound City.

When we settled in front of the counter, Buckskin Compton wiped the sweat off his brow, took a deep breath, and after he exhaled, nodded at the red-headed gal in front of us, and asked for a big glass of water and some coffee and a doughnut, which he called a bear-sign, a word I'd heard some cowboys use. I ordered what Buckskin was having.

"Nice bat," he said, but it felt like he meant something else.

I looked down at my bat, then up and around, and I saw that just about everybody else in the pastry shop was looking at it, too. So I leaned it against the counter so nobody might get the impression it was a weapon and go calling on Sheriff Roodhouse.

It was a nice bat. One of the newer kinds, big and heavy, white ash, with four red stripes about where the rosin ended, and a big fat red stripe between the small rounded knob—about the size of a good tomato—at the end of the handle, but that stripe wasn't as shiny on account of all the rosin and pine tar I'd rubbed there to keep the bat from slipping in my hands while I was batting. There was another red stripe, nowhere near as big as the one by the handle but maybe the size of two of the four down below, and one final red stripe, same size as the last one I mentioned, right at the top of the bat.

"You swing it well," Buckskin said. "You sure you really want to swing it dressed in bloomers?"

We waited till the redhead served our orders and wandered to the far end of the counter to talk to a fat girl and her bespectacled brunette friend in a polka dot dress.

"Well . . . you do it," I said.

"I have my reasons."

"But I ain't wearing no wig."

He bit into his doughnut, wiped the powder from his lips. "Yeah, that's what you told Ed. When's the last time you had your hair cut?"

That had been right after Pa died when the Widow Amy DeFee made me do it so I'd look "presentable" at the funeral.

"Back in Mound City, it sounded like you wanted me to play . . ."—it struck me how little time had passed—"just yesterday."

"Don't let this go to your head, kid, but you're too good a ballist to be playing for a bunch of frauds."

"You ain't bad yourself."

He smiled. "But I am a fraud."

We ate in silence, and Buckskin insisted on paying for my coffee and bear-sign, and said we might as well go over and see if Mr. Norris had sobered up.

He had. We found him at the baseball field, which wasn't no pasture. The Bloomers' crew was scurrying around, setting up the canvas fences along with the grandstand. Mr. Norris was right happy to see me, and even happier to learn that I was an orphan so he didn't have to hear no gab from an angry mother like he did when Ruth Eagan's ma got to complaining.

The mention of Ruth's ma made Ed Norris snap his finger.

"This is the most important thing, kid," he told me. "Listen, on your own time, I don't care what you do, or anything like that. Find a petticoat. Find an opium den. Whatever suits you. But any time you're around Ruth Eagan, you're a gal. Get it. You're Lucy Totton. And he's Dolly Madison. And Nelse is Nellie. And Russ is Lady Waddell. Don't ask me to explain it. You'd have to get your brains wrapped around the way her shatterpated ma thinks. Even when you're on the train, when Ruth's around, the bloomers stay on and so does the wig. 'Course, you don't need a wig. But when's the last time you washed that hair? Do that. Like now. Have you checked out, Buckskin? If not, get him back to the hotel. Get him cleaned up. Where's your luggage? Never mind . . . ," he stopped and half turned to shout at the workers over in right-center field. "You idiot! That's not an iron rod, it's a two-by-four." He started walking that way but paused to yell at Buckskin: "Get him dressed and ready! Get the dirt off his face! Redden his lips. And be back here ninety minutes before the game starts!"

Well, that's how I started playing for the National Bloomer Girls. We lost, 10-to-8, to the Fort Scott Athletics, but we had them down by one run in the seventh. We lost to Galesburg on Monday, 4-to-2. Got rained out in Thayer.

Then we were on the train, rocking and swaying, to some other city, and some other game. And I was listening to Buckskin Compton and Nelse McConnell and Mr. Norris—mostly Mr. Norris talking and Buckskin and Nelse listening—saying that he never should have played that game in Fort Scott.

"That scoundrel of a reporter. He's a muck-raker." He held up a copy of the *Tribune and Monitor* and began reading: "'Three of the men were in men's suits.' That's a shameless falsehood. You were all in bloomers and wigs. '. . . the first baseman, shortstop, pitcher, and right fielder were men.' Another lie. The battery were men. They always are. But who could mistake Ruth Eagan for a boy? No man'd ever take a catcher's mitt to play first base. It oughtn't even be allowed for dames."

I'd never mistake Ruth for a fellow. To me

55

she was real pretty, which I might've already mentioned.

"If I recall," Buckskin said, "that Fort Scott newspaper said we played before a thousand people."

"So what?" Mr. Norris belted out.

"Twenty-five cents a head . . . that's two hundred and fifty dollars, which leaves you one hundred and eighty-seven dollars and fifty cents. That doesn't include programs sold, which all goes to the National Bloomer Girls, and the split in concessions. Or our *appearance* fee."

"You done all that ciphering in your head?" McConnell asked in pure amazement.

Buckskin grinned. "It doesn't take into account the bets you placed, either, Ed."

"It also doesn't take into account what I pay *you*," Mr. Norris said. "Or those idiots to put up and take down the grandstand and fences. And I don't place bets. I sure wouldn't bet on this team of dunderheads."

"I didn't say you bet on us," Buckskin said, but Mr. Norris didn't hear. His mouth was running like a thoroughbred.

"This train isn't free. This women's team will drive me to the poor house yet."

"You pay us a decent wage," Buckskin said. "You pay the girls something else." Only it wasn't *something else* Buckskin said. "And we've drawn bigger crowds than we did at Fort Scott."

"Yeah," McConnell said. "The newspaper kid I talked to said folks have never supported baseball in that town."

"You talked to a newspaperman?" Mr. Norris belted out. "I told you never to talk to a news-paperman. *I* talk to the press. Did you tell that reporter that some players weren't ladies?"

"A kid," McConnell explained. "A boy selling papers. Not a reporter. Unless they let nine-year-olds write for them."

Mr. Norris gulped down what was left in his flask. "A story like that'll ruin us."

"It's one paper, boss," McConnell told the manager.

"That's what you think," Mr. Norris came back at him. "Ever heard of a stagecoach? A train . . . like the one we're riding . . . or the invention of the telegraph? It's starting to seem that every town we play in has picked up that pack of lies printed in that Fort Scott paper."

"Not just lies, boss," Buckskin said. "We are men."

"Balderdash." Again, that ain't exactly the word Mr. Norris spoke.

Now that he mentioned it, it struck me how right Mr. Norris was. You see, I'd been reading them newspapers, too, as best I could, or at least looking over them to see if there were any reports about a runaway from Pleasanton—nothing—or, even better, the arrest or shooting down of two

57

murdering scoundrels in Pleasanton, meaning the Widow Amy DeFee and Judge Brett.

No luck. No stories like that. Just a bunch of boring stuff, and some baseball scores and write-ups, and, yes, sir-ree, a paragraph or two about the Bloomer Girls being men and girls that had been first printed in that Fort Scott newspaper.

Then as Mr. Norris was rampaging against the press, I realized that that sorry reporter hadn't said the second baseman was a man, and I'd been playing second base.

I was about to say something about that, but that train kept right on rocking, and the next thing I knew, Buckskin was poking my shoulder to wake me, saying that we was at wherever we was to play another game.

CHAPTER FIVE

The Bloomer Girls do not expect
to draw crowds entirely on
account of the novelty of being
lady base ball players, but
really put up a very creditable
game. They travel in a private
palace car and carry a canvas
fence 14 feet high and 1200 ft.
long for enclosing the grounds,
a canopy covered grandstand with
a capacity of 2000, and everything necessary to give a first
class exhibition. They have
toured every state, also Canada,
and have everywhere received
good notices from the press, not
only for their good base ball
playing, but also for their lady-
like behavior.

The Evening News
Ada, Indian Territory
July 20, 1906

It was a right nice train. We had Pullman
sleepers for our team. Didn't share them with
no folks on the regular run. Had our own smoking

room, even though I never saw no need in rolling dead grass into a piece of paper, then lighting one end and then sucking on that burning paper.

I was learning the rules, like them written down on a paper we all had to sign:

- √ No kicking, quarreling, or demonstrative criticisms while traveling on train, stagecoach, omnibus or any public or private conveyance, or at depots or hotels. Offending party is subject to pay a fine of 20 cents for each offense.
- √ No flirting, mashing, or making the acquaintance of any gentleman on trains, steamboats, or any public or private conveyance, or at depots, hotels, restaurants, or any public place. Offending party is subject to pay a fine of between 25 cents and $3, depending on the severity of the offense.
- √ No receiving of any notes from any gentleman with mashing on his mind. Offending party is subject to a fine of 25 cents.
- √ No entering, either during daylight or nighttime, any saloon, barroom, gambling den, grog shop, winery, or any establishment where intoxicating beverages are sold. Offending party is subject to a fine of no less than 50 cents and no more than $2.

√ No digressing from the proper places for ladies, which are in their rooms at their hotels or in the ladies parlor, and no running through or occupying a hotel office or a gentleman's sitting or waiting room. Offending party is subject to a fine of no less than 25 cents and no more than 50 cents.

Them rules, Buckskin told me, didn't apply to us on account we wasn't ladies.

The thing you got to remember is that I'd spent most of my baseball career traveling from one field to another on my Hawthorne. Now I was riding on a train, as was my bike, though I was mostly sleeping on account it's right hard to stay awake with a coach swaying this way and that, and the iron wheels making that noise that sounded to most folks like clickety-clack but to me sounded like Go-To-Sleep-Go-To-Sleep.

That's what I'd done. We had played some team in some town. After about a week of baseball games practically every day, and sometimes two a day, games and towns and catches and hits and errors, not to mention wins and losses, sort of run together. We'd played two games, and that cool spell that had been hovering over Kansas had gone somewhere else, and Kansas had reverted back to its hot, windy ways, and that's why I was so plumb tuckered that when I settled into a chair in our parlor car, I was sleeping like a dead man. When I felt someone nudge me, I yawned and muttered something, slowly opened my eyes, and . . .

There she was, sitting right across from me.

"We didn't mean to wake you," Ruth Eagan said.

I blinked, and saw Mrs. Eagan standing right over me, that perpetual scowl saying that I'd better not get no notions as she knew that I wasn't no girl.

"It's . . ." I stopped, dragged my shoes off the bench, and tried not to sound like a sixteen-year-old boy, though Buckskin, who weren't a real deep talker hisself, said I didn't have to worry about my voice till it finally got around to changing, and even after that occurrence I wasn't never going to sing in no mezzo-soprano voice or be another Edyth Walker, which I still ain't rightly figured out what that means or what Bloomer team Edyth Walker plays for.

"It's all right." I was still donned in my bloomers. My baseball bat and glove lay on the hard seat next to me.

"Mother's getting some tea and cookies," Ruth Eagan said. "Would you like some?"

"Well, sure." See, I wasn't thinking clear, but the look Mrs. Eagan give me told me she weren't right happy about nothing, and then Ruth was sliding into the seat across from me and saying something to her ma, whose eyes bore through me like she was the Widow Amy DeFee come for killing.

Finally, after leaving me with one more scowl, Mrs. Eagan moved down the rocking aisle toward that bar at the front of the parlor car where the National Bloomer Girls organization had all sorts of drinks—not intoxicating spirits, mind you—and cakes and cookies and nuts. Every now and then there's be sandwiches or soups, but not on this particular run.

Ruth grinned, pulled up her skirts, and moved from the seat across from me to right next to me. I had to slide over some, and put my baseball bat on the seat where Ruth had been sitting.

"This way I can keep my eye on Mother." She got this look of pure contentment, like my face must've gotten any time I figured out a way to do something spiteful to the Widow Amy DeFee. She raised her right hand and gave a little wave to her ma.

"Wonderful," Ruth whispered.

"What?" I pretended to be staring out the window watching the Kansas scenery go roaring by at twenty miles an hour.

"The man has to heat up water for our tea."

Ruth had gotten out of her Bloomer Girls uniform and was dressed in a skirt of navy blue and a blouse that was a lighter blue with little print of different colored roses, and a belt pulled real tight around her waist that seemed to accentuate—Ruth used that word some time later, probably the first time *accentuate* was ever uttered aloud in Topeka—her . . . ummm, well . . . the ruffles around the top of her blouse, and those sleeves that was puffed up something extraordinaire from her shoulders to her elbows. She was busy opening her big bag and talking at the same time, every few seconds glancing up and smiling at her ma, but I figured she was just checking on the exact location of Mrs. Eagan.

"You like to read, don't you, Lucy?"

Didn't have no time to answer, on account she was saying: "I know you do. I see you all the time going through newspapers. Mother never lets me read newspapers. Says they're nothing for a proper lady to read. In fact, she doesn't think a lady should be reading at all . . . not even the Bible. That's for the pastor to read to us and tell us what it means. So I have to read anything I can, and wait . . ." She checked on her mother before pulling out a fair-sized book. She lifted it ever so discreetly so that I could see the cover, which was brown with red letters, all caps, and some design in the center that took me a while to figure out, but then, as my reading went, so did figuring out the title.

"Have you read this?" Ruth asked, again not waiting for an answer. "Of course you have. Everyone has. But here's what I keep reading over and over and over again. Here." She thrust the book at me.

My eyes landed on the full-page drawing next to the page which had nothing but words. It was a right fair drawing of some cowboys in a darkened room playing cards, and there was some writing underneath it that caught my attention, just as Ruth was quoting, from memory: " 'Therefore Trampas spoke. Your bet, you son-of-a- . . .' "

She said the whole word. But when I read it, I seen that Trampas didn't. The last part of that there bad word on page twenty-nine was just a long dash.

Giggling, she took the book back and shoved it into her purse. "Oh, how I wish the Bloomer Girls could play a baseball game in Wyoming."

At least she give me time enough to read the title. "Because of *The Virginian*?" I asked.

Ruth waved her hand. "Oh, heavens no. I like the idea of Owen Wister's hero, though I found Trampas more exciting, and Steve . . ." She stopped to do some tsk-tsk-ing. "Such a tragic figure. And the West. It's grand. It's adventurous. Exciting. Cowboys are so dashing and fun and lively. I can't wait till we play in Dodge City. Yet still." Her head tilted back. "But it's Wyoming. Wyoming." She said it like some folks say the ocean, or the Rocky Mountains, or bacon. "We have the vote in Wyoming. Always have."

"We do?" I said.

"Yes. And soon we women won't just be voting or holding office in Wyoming, but across these United States. We'll be playing baseball, too. The men will no longer dominate." Her head shook. "Wister's Molly is such a weakling. She reminds me of my older sister. But Wister isn't a woman, so he doesn't know what we feel. In fact, I'm not overwhelmed by his gift of prose, but . . ." She leaned forward, lowered her voice, and quoted the line again, whole and complete!

"With whom are you bunking?" she asked me after a pause. "Mother hasn't told me."

"Ummm. Buck . . . I mean . . . ummm . . ."

"It doesn't matter. When we move north in four days, we'll have to change trains to board the Santa Fe. So, when that happens, they'll send us to a Harvey House for supper. We've made arrangements to discuss important matters. Suffrage. Putting women everywhere. Susan B. Anthony might be dead now, but we are united behind her cause." Her voice changed. "You played very well today," she told me.

"Oh. Thank you. And you . . . ummm . . ." Must've still been more asleep, and now completely confused about suffrage and Owen Wister, and the sound of Ruth Eagan's voice when she said son-of-a-.

"I did a fine job of selling programs." Now Ruth sounded sarcastic, but her mother was back, holding a tray that held cups of piping hot tea and cookies and tiny bites of cake.

I tried to stand up, remembering to be a gentleman whenever possible, and stopped halfway up because I wasn't sure it was proper for a girl to help a mean-eyed woman. But Mrs. Eagan's glare sent me settling back down into my seat. Ruth got up and took the tray and then she got into a discussion with her ma, who, turns out, didn't think it was proper for ladies to be selling programs at baseball fields. That went on for quite a while, till I shut them both up by asking a question.

"But a woman can play baseball?"

Right then I knew that Mrs. Eagan despised my guts as much as did the Widow Amy DeFee.

"*Touché.* Wonderful, Lucy. A marvelous comeback," Ruth said, and lifted her cup and clinked it against mine. "Let me tell you about Mother," Ruth said. "There are some things a woman should do, many things a woman sha'n't do, but Mother's sister, my Aunt Jessica, attended Vassar and played baseball there. Aunt Jessica says that I have talent, that I can play as well as many male players, and when Father found out what the National Bloomer Girls are willing to pay . . ."

"Enough." Mrs. Eagan sounded just like the Widow Amy DeFee, and I spilt some of my tea.

"You swing the bat good," I told Ruth.

"Not as well as you do," she said.

I shrugged and told her: "You play good."

"Well," Mrs. Eagan said.

I looked at her, and waited. I knew that when someone says *well* they generally go on to say something they find right important, but she just looked at me like I was an idiot.

Sighing, she said: "You play *well*. Not . . . you play *good*."

Ruth laughed, and then she leaned over to me and whispered, and her eyes shined with hope and a longing to hear something that she wanted to hear so bad. What she whispered was: "Do you think I can play baseball as well as any man?"

"Ruth Eagan," her ma reprimanded.

I was getting sleepy again because the train was really rocking and now I had a belly full of cookies, puny slices of cake, and some tea, and I wasn't thinking real straight. But Ruth being so close, and me smelling that fresh soap at her throat and thinking that maybe what she wanted to hear was the truth, I decided to tell her.

"Not when you're playing first base wearing a catcher's mitt."

I watched the look on Ruth's face change as she slammed back into her chair. Then I looked over at Ruth's ma and saw her beaming and happy, like she'd been drinking some Oh-Be-Joyful and not hot tea. I felt like I'd gotten kicked in my belly, and I knew that must've been how Ruth felt on account that I'd dashed all her dreams.

I wanted to say how sorry I was, because tears welled in her eyes. I sure wished Buckskin was sitting next to me because he could be right savvy and he could've figured out what would change everything that had suddenly turned out so awful wrong.

Didn't happen though.

What happened was Ruth shot up suddenly, left her cup in the tray that was sitting next to Mrs. Eagan, and she didn't look at me at all, just said curtly to her mother: "Let's go." She started for the door toward the Pullman where we ballists sleep.

Mrs. Eagan daintily put her cup on that tray, and rose like a real lady, giving me a look that didn't need no words.

All alone, I felt like a louse.

Which, Buckskin later told me, was how I should've felt.

Chapter Six

The National Bloomer Girls, in jumpers and baggy knee pants, are to play ball here next Friday. It will be remembered that there was a "bloomer girl" crowd here last year, but the fans kicked because some of the "girls" were masculine gender and wore long golden locks, while some of the players didn't even pretend to ally themselves with the fair sex. It is hoped the National bloomer management will at least bring a bona fide aggregation to town whether they can play the National game or not.

Toronto Republican
Toronto, Kansas
May 17, 1906

There ain't really nothing worser than getting shoved awake out of a miserable sleep when your bones ache, and you got a crick in your neck, and then you up and let out a scream on account your first thoughts is that the Widow Amy DeFee has found you.

"Gosh darn it, kid," a voice throttled way down in some dark tunnel, "what the heck's got into you?"

Yeah, you'd be right if you're guessing that Buckskin Compton didn't actually say *gosh darn* or *heck*.

The only good thing that I could notice was that it wasn't Judge Brett or the widow standing by my seat, but Buckskin Compton. It was also good I hadn't messed my bloomers.

"Oh." I looked out the window and saw nothing but lanterns glowing and the shadows of figures heading down the depot's platform and vanishing in the dark 'cause, as I learnt ten minutes later, it was three-thirty in the morning. "Where are we?"

"Toronto," Buckskin said.

"Canada?" Joy entered my heart, by grab, knowing that the Widow Amy DeFee and her murdering judge wasn't never going to find me up here.

Buckskin muttered a few more salty words. Reckon he wasn't too happy to be awake at that hour, neither. "Toronto, Kansas."

"Oh."

"Come on, kid," Buckskin said. "We're going to the hotel for a few hours."

Blinking and yawning, I slowly come close to being awake. Buckskin had set a couple of bags on the seat across the aisle, but he kept holding this long, slender one that I'd seen him carry to every game we ever played. And now when I thought more about it, I'd seen him carrying that bag just about everywhere he went, even to the privy a time or two. Now professional ballists feel a mother's love toward their baseball bats, and that thought made me make sure no thief had made off with mine, which remained on the slatted rack above my seat. After rubbing the sleep out of my eyes, I focused on Buckskin.

And his dress, apron, and wig.

"Got your grip?" Buckskin asked.

"Ummm." I pointed over my head at the sack that rested against my ash bat.

"That's what I thought," Buckskin said. "Get it, and let's go."

Buckskin didn't even let me close my eyes once we got up to the room we shared with Nelson "Nellie" McConnell and Russ "Lady" Waddell, neither being really pleased with Buckskin ordering a tub and hot water be brought up to the room after we registered downstairs. It was still the wee hours of the morning.

"Gee willikins." Yes, Russ Waddell actually used that word. "Can't a bath wait?" He did add some adjectives—or is them adverbs?—in front of *wait,* though.

McConnell muttered something, too, but for some reason his cussing reminded me of some night song my ma—my real ma, not my other ma, that hydrophoby dog called the Widow Amy DeFee—used to sing to me so I would go to sleep. Three, four cusses was all it took before McConnell began snoring in one of the two beds.

Waddell fetched a bottle from his grip while this big fellow with flaxen hair poured buckets of hot water into the tub that had been rolled in and set between the two beds on account that was about the only place you could fit a tub in a room maybe a little bit bigger than that four-seater behind that Missouri Pacific depot that was marked **LADIES ONLY**, and that we had visited before coming into the hotel. We had had to wait the most awfullest long time on account the Bloomer Girls were with us, along with some other ladies who were either getting off in Toronto or didn't want to use the facilities in the coaches no more. Anyway, 'cause we were still dressed in our uniforms or, like Waddell and Buckskin, in dresses and wigs, we couldn't go into the men's two-seater where there weren't hardly nobody waiting at all.

"Will that do, sir?" the flaxen-haired kid asked in a funny accent that Buckskin later told me was Norwegian.

"We'll see," Buckskin said, as he tipped the boy and closed the door behind him. Looking at me, he pointed at the steaming tub, and ordered—bossing like Ed Norris done most of the time—"Get in."

My mean look didn't scare him none.

"You stink," Waddell said as he pulled off his dress.

Weren't nothing wrong with my nose. Or my eyes, neither, 'cause a quick glance around that room revealed that there wasn't no screen so a body could have privacy. Wasn't nothing but a dresser, a chamber pot, and a mirror. The mirror was cracked and the chamber pot wasn't exactly spotless. I got undressed.

The hot, soapy water felt good, but the feeling left once I spied Buckskin opening my sack.

"You stop that," I told him. "That's my stuff."

He dropped my leather ball glove onto the bed, but my stockings got pitched into the tub, whilst Waddell, holding the small bottle in his left hand, used his right to dunk my uniform under water, too. Everything, excepting my shoes. Then Waddell submerged his left hand in the water, shook it off some, and dried it on McConnell's Bloomer Girls' shirt.

My plans were to step out of the portable tub and have a go at fisticuffs, but Buckskin shook his finger, then pointed at the floor. "You ruin that rug, the hotel manager will charge Norris for damages and Norris'll take it out of your pay."

So I sank back into the tub, but not 'cause I didn't want to lose a penny of the money I was supposed to be getting paid. Besides, that hot, soapy water did feel good.

"Blue Buckles," Buckskin said as threw my overalls into the darkening water. "And whatever this once was."

"That's one of my three-for-a-dollar shirts," I said, feeling sort of embarrassed.

"The other two must have been the forty-five-cent ones, 'cause this one ain't worth more than a dime," Waddell commented, corking his bottle and throwing it to Buckskin, who took the cork out with his teeth and splashed some of them ardent spirits on the hand he'd used to throw my duds into the tub. After drying his hand on McConnell's Bloomer Girls' shirt, he plucked the cork from his teeth and took himself a swallow of liquor.

"A prince's wardrobe," Buckskin said after McConnell finished muttering some cusses between snores and grunts like a fat hog might make and rolled over. Buckskin handed the bottle back to Waddell, and called me a "runaway."

"I don't think he's an Army deserter," Waddell said after taking a sip from the bottle.

Forgetting all about my clothes that was getting washed, or being called a runaway, a thought got me nervous, and I shouted out: "Toronto!"

"Huh?" they said.

"Where do we go next?" I asked, having realized that after all the baseball games I'd been playing, I wasn't no more than a hundred miles from where the Widow Amy DeFee and Judge Brett were living.

"Emporia, I think," Waddell said after a long staring session with Buckskin.

That was better, I thought. More north, more west from Pleasanton.

"And after that?" I asked.

"You'll be sorry when you see me in Toledo," McConnell mumbled in his sleep, coherent and clear like he was wide awake and not drunk, neither of which he was.

"Chanute," Buckskin said.

Which was worser. Even closer to Pleasanton than Toronto. When you play baseball as a ringer for teams across the state, you come to know a little bit about geography.

My stomach started rumbling, which caused me to fart—which I do when I get nervous—and that made the water bubble. That got Waddell to laugh but Buckskin just stared harder at me and scratched his head, meaning, of course, his real hair, not the wig he put on to fool the Bloomer Girls, the crowds, but *not* too many reporters.

"We aren't going to play a game in . . ." I stopped, looked at my two teammates, and quickly knew I'd better not mention Pleasanton, scairt that might get them to learning the truth and they'd tell Mr. Norris that I wasn't an orphan but a runaway, even though I happened to be both. But iffen we wound up in Pleasanton, I'd be deader than the Boston Beaneaters already was in the National League.

So I said: "Kansas City." Which was stupid, and not what I meant to say, which was Yates City, which was also in Woodson County. Besides, Yates City didn't have no baseball team, I'd ever played for or against. I really didn't know nothing about that town, which might have been why I said Kansas City by mistake, but it didn't matter what I said, 'cause Buckskin kept right on staring at me.

"You *are* a runaway!" Buckskin shouted, which got him to cussing, which got Ed Norris, in the room next to ours, pounding against the wall and telling us to get some sleep 'cause we got a game to play at two in the afternoon.

Waddell kept trying to sink his head deeper into his pillow, but his pillow was like a brick, which added to his irritableness, so he snapped at Buckskin: "What difference does it make if he's a runaway? He plays good ball for a kid his age."

"He joined us in Fort Scott," Buckskin said, keeping his voice down 'cause just before he said that Mr. Norris had banged on the wall again and said that if we didn't shut up and go to bed, he was going to start implementing fines for disobeying the going-to-sleep rule. I didn't recollect reading about no going-to-sleep rule, but I guess we could've been fined for kicking, quarreling, or causing a commotion when we were supposed to be sleeping.

"He brings nothing but a bicycle, gear, and the clothes on his back," Buckskin muttered to himself. Which made me pray that the fellows that traveled with us and did all the constructing of our baseball stands and fences remembered to take good care of my Hawthorne, which they'd been real good at so far. Still it was starting to look to me like I'd have to be leaving the National Bloomer Girls before the sun rose, and pedaling as fast and as far away from the Widow Amy DeFee and Judge Brett as I could.

"Maybe he's poor," Waddell said, like I wasn't right there. "Have you seen most of the rubes who come to our games, Buckskin?"

"I don't want the law to come down on us 'cause we're traveling with a runaway," Buckskin said.

"The law won't," Waddell said. " 'Cause if Nelse finds out, he'll turn him in for the reward. And if Nelse doesn't, Norris sure will."

"I'm not a runaway." Yes, I was, but there wasn't nothing illegal about running away from a couple of murderers. "Both of my parents are dead," I told them. That was, sadly, truthful.

"I wanted to run away and join the circus," McConnell said as he rolled over. "Still do, sometimes." We looked at him, but he started snoring again.

Waddell laughed.

But me and Buckskin didn't.

"Give the kid a break," Waddell said. "We're all running away from something."

Buckskin sat down on his bed and held out his hand to Waddell, wanting what was left of the whiskey. Waddell obliged. Buckskin drained the bottle, and then he laid his head down on his rock-hard pillow and didn't say nothing no more.

CHAPTER SEVEN

Every Tuesday and Thursday evening
the Normal girls play baseball
on the Normal athletic field,
behind closed gates. With field
glasses you can get a good view
of the surrounding country from
Perley's hill, or on the east
side of the field for the fence
is down.

The Emporia Gazette
Emporia, Kansas
June 24, 1906

Before I got paid a lot more than four or six bits to play baseball, it typically took two, three weeks before I forgot how good I had done—extra-base hits, super catches, things like that. But errors, strikeouts, and bone-head plays I had made would stick in my craw much longer. But you got to understand that way back then, I'd have a game once, twice a week, unless we got a couple of doubleheaders. Now that I was traveling by train and playing practically every day, albeit in bloomers, well, the point I'm making is that I honestly ain't got nary a clue how we played in Toronto, how I did, what the rival team was like, or what the town was like. Nothing at all. It's like the only thing that happened in Toronto occurred at that rawhide hotel between four and five-thirty that morning. Can't recollect lots of other games, or towns, neither.

Emporia. Now that town I remember. Quite well. The town, I mean. Not the game. 'Cause there weren't no game.

"What do you mean?" Mr. Ed Norris was saying when me and Buckskin arrived at the city's baseball field. He wasn't talking to us, but to this weasel in a straw hat and spectacles pushed far down his crooked nose. Behind him stood four, five fellows bigger than some fat steers I'd seen in cattle cars bound for to the Kansas City packing houses.

"The contract said we were to play the National Bloomer Girls," said the straw-hatted weasel, emphasizing the word *girls*.

"And I am manager of the National Bloomer Girls," Mr. Norris said. "You will be playing the Bloomer Girls."

The weasel pointed at me. "Girls? Mister, I sure ain't fondling that witch." But he didn't say *fondling* or *witch*.

"I don't know, Vern," said one of the ruffians behind him. "The little one's sexful. Very sexful indeed."

Them other tough *hombres* took to sniggering, and my face turned redder than a fresh-popped blister after the dead skin's got ripped off. See, we wasn't in our Bloomer Girls uniform. Buckskin and me had gotten up before all the girls, gotten up before Waddell and McConnell, too, but that usually happened. We'd left the hotel with Buckskin dressed in plaid trousers and a bib-front shirt and me wearing the duds that I'd worn to Mound City which had at least got washed in that tub in Toronto.

"But the other?" The big bruiser eyed Buckskin, then immediately shut up and the sniggering stopped on account that Buckskin give all of them one of his I'm-a-mad-dog-killer looks.

But Mr. Norris and that fellow Vern kept right on arguing. The weasel saying he wasn't going to risk losing a game to girls that wasn't really girls at all, even though most of us were girls—just not me and Buckskin or Lady Waddell or Nellie McConnell. After all, it takes nine players to field a baseball team and us fellows totaled only four. So most of us were girls, just not us, you see.

Anyway, Mr. Norris refused to return the advance he had got paid, or his appearance fee— since he did show up—and that explained how come he had that shiner surrounding his left eye when we seen him later that afternoon.

Buckskin said to me: "Let's go." So the two of us left the baseball field and didn't come back on account there wasn't no game that day. But Mr.

Norris stayed, which is how come his eye got black by the time we seen him next.

Having gotten paid, Buckskin, carrying his bat bag and a smaller grip with his glove and uniform, led me to a tonsorial parlor called The Elk Barber Shop where he got shaved.

"Close," he told the barber. "Real close."

So I told another of the three barbers in that shop that I'd like me a shave, too, but Buckskin said that I couldn't have no shave. Seems he thought it might cause my face to break out and then I wouldn't look like some virginal goddess no more, which got all three of the barbers and two gents waiting for their shaves and haircuts laughing mighty hard. All it got me was a red face.

But I didn't hold no grudge too long since after his shave, Buckskin took me to Tiffany's Corner Bakery, and, by golly, the bread loafs they dished out was about as long as my bat. After that we went to do some shopping. I wanted to go to this place with this fancy-dressed guy in a newspaper advertisement pasted on the front door, but Buckskin just kept on walking.

I ended up spending most of my first pay at G.W. Newman's Dry Goods Co.—they was having a sale. Can't complain too much, I reckon. Buckskin let me pick out a boy's suit for three dollars and forty-nine cents, a pair of dollar seventy-five shoes that was on sale for ninety-eight cents, undergarments, socks, some everyday trousers and two shirts. Then we wandered over to the ladies area, Buckskin saying real loud that my ma's birthday was coming up, which turned me sad 'cause it started me thinking about my real ma, Gertrude Grace. I knew what we was buying was for me on account Buckskin held up a black mercerized—whatever that meant—skirt to my waist.

"She's about your size, I do believe," Buckskin said as he measured that skirt against me, aware of a gray-haired lady holding up her spectacles as she stared in our direction. "Can't believe how big you've grown. Tall as your mother already," he said in an excited, loud voice.

The old lady lowered her glasses, made herself smile, but she still kept glancing over her shoulder whilst Buckskin tossed some female unmentionables, a wrap, some dress linings, a bonnet, and some other girlie stuff in my arms.

I had to pay for all that, too. Buckskin sprung for a lady's valise, where he stored some of my new female clothes, and then said that he'd buy me dinner, not that I was very hungry after eating that big loaf of bread we'd chowed down earlier.

We walked down the boardwalk in the direction of the hotel, me carrying a few packages wrapped in brown paper and tied up with twine in one hand and the valise and a sack of baseball gear in the other. Suddenly, Buckskin shoved me down an alley we was passing, and leaped in right behind me. He pushed me against the wall and he brung up that baseball bat bag, holding his breath as he whispered for me not to say nothing, not to even breathe. He kept his eye on two fellows—who looked pretty much like the drawings I'd seen in Owen Wister's *The Virginian*—as they slowly rode their ponies down Cunningham Street.

After they'd gone out of sight, and once me and Buckskin could breathe again, we sprung out of that alley and didn't stop till Buckskin hurried me inside this place called **Haynes Brothers'**, according to the sign. Inside, a puny man wearing a visor and apron looked up and laid a big old Remington revolver on the counter. I jumped back, but then saw that the cylinder wasn't even in the pistol and the barrel had a stick poking down it. Don't think he thought we meant to rob him, which sure seemed to be what Buckskin had in mind as hard and as fast as he opened and slammed the door and shoved me inside.

"I'd like a box of Forty-Five-Nineties," Buckskin said, after he nodded at the man.

The little man pushed back his visor. "That's a mighty big caliber, mister. Ain't what most folks shoot around here . . . now that the buffalo's all gone."

I think the man was trying for a joke, but Buckskin's brusk *yeah* let him know that he wasn't interested in funny.

"I'll have to look in the back to see if I got any," the fellow said.

Four minutes later, he come back with a box that he was wiping dust from with a handkerchief before setting it atop the counter near the register. He excused himself as he thumbed through papers underneath the register to find out the price of a box of .45-90 shells. He had trouble 'cause whilst he had been in the storeroom getting the shells meant for hunting battleships or elephants, Buckskin had drawn down the shades on the door and one of the big windows.

"Is there anything else, sir?" the man asked whilst wetting his lips with his tongue and glancing at the shades.

"No . . ." Buckskin stopped and stepped back to study the revolvers and other manly things displayed inside the glass case.

"How much for the Lightning? And that pair of binoculars?"

Maybe twenty minutes later, Buckskin stuck the revolver in the waistband at his back, which his jacket covered. The shells he put inside his baseball bat bag. The spyglasses he give me to carry, which I hung around my neck. He thanked the man, and on his way out the door, Buckskin pulled the shades back up. Then he looked up and down the street before he come full out onto the boardwalk. Almost like we was trying to beat out a weak roller back to the mound, we returned to the Nutting Hotel.

We went up the back staircase, real sneaky. Since Buckskin told me not to say one word, I didn't ask how come, being savvy enough to figure out that it didn't have nothing to do with the fact that pretty Ruth Eagan might see us not outfitted like Bloomers or girls.

Things got even stranger once inside our room. He locked the door. Waddell and McConnell wasn't in the room. I figured they was either out drinking or looking for a card game since McConnell had bragged that he and Waddell, dressed as Bloomers, had made some money playing poker on the train ride from Toledo. Seems the two had sat with a couple of businessmen in the smoking car who were in their cups. They drank with them until the two was out cold, then Waddell relieved them of all their greenbacks. They used that money to play cards with two other gents who thought they was teaching poker to the two girls. Them fellows couldn't scarcely believe the luck those two had playing poker for the first time.

"Get dressed," Buckskin ordered me, after we had been in the room less than ten minutes. He tossed me a skirt, looking like he wasn't gonna brook no argument.

After we got all duded up like women, we walked to the Normal school.

• • •

Sitting on Perley's hill, Buckskin used his new binoculars to watch some young ladies as they practiced baseball.

"I know what you're thinking, kid," Buckskin said, "but this isn't Coventry, those aren't Lady Godivas, and I'm no peeping Tom."

Didn't know what he was talking about. Still don't. Just before I wrote that there sentence, Buckskin told me I'd have to learn that for myself. Maybe I will, someday.

What I, a sixteen-year-old, was thinking at that particular time on that day was that it sure weren't fair that, up here and pretty much out of sight, Buckskin, at least ten years older than me and maybe as much as twenty, got to watch girls at the Normal school play baseball through binoculars whilst I just used my eyes. Perley's hill might not be no mountain, us still being in Kansas, but it was still a right far piece to watch girls run the bases or bend over to scoop up soft rollers in the infield.

When I tired of straining my eyes, I found something else to hold my attention and it got me to thinking.

A ladies' pocketbook lay between Buckskin's legs, and it was open so I had a good view of them ivory grips of his new Lightning revolver, and I knew why he brung it and left his skinny bat bag under our bed at the Nutting Hotel. A lady in a poke-shaped bonnet, cotton blouse, and skirt hauling a long, heavy thin bag would draw too much attention. I'd told Buckskin that I could cart them binoculars in the sack that once held all my regular duds, but he made me put them spyglasses in my new valise. The valise wouldn't get much attention, neither.

Two women sitting on a hill watching girls practice baseball, I also reckoned, wouldn't result in no lynching unless they was discovered to be a man and a boy.

I didn't ask Buckskin why he was spying on the Normal baseball girls. Wasn't sure I wanted to know.

But one thing I'd already figured out, having seen that Lightning in the pocketbook and understanding that his long bag carried a .45-90 rifle as well as baseball bats.

Yep, Russ Waddell had spoke the truth the other night when he'd said: "We're all running away from something."

CHAPTER EIGHT

The National Bloomer Girls base
ball team of Kansas City will
play the Eagles at Athletic Park
next Monday, May 28. The "girls"
are said to play a good game
of base ball and have a record
of winning games. The team is
composed of all girls and the
pitcher is a wonder. . . . Those
who think a woman cannot throw
a ball straight will be greatly
surprised at the excellent game
the Bloomer Girls put up.

The Sun
Chanute, Kansas
May 24, 1906

Hold your hand out, palm toward me,"
Buckskin ordered.

In another hotel room, in another town, we were
getting dressed for the game against Chanute. I'd
been looking at my fingernails 'cause Mr. Norris
asked me to pitch this game and let Russ "Lady"
Waddell rest his arm. I give Buckskin a funny
look, but did like he told me.

"Spread your fingers out."

90

When I done that, Buckskin nodded. "That's how a woman looks at her nails."

"Huh?"

Buckskin laughed. "You were bending your fingers toward you, looking at your nails. That's how men look at their nails. One of the differences between men and women. Usually. Not always. But usually."

I went back to studying my nails the way I usually done on account that I ain't no female.

"That's a good way to arouse suspicion." Buckskin sounded and looked right serious.

Not that I had to do this, but I took in everything that was in the room—the other bed, the dresser, the wash basin, our grips, Buckskin's bat bag that held a .45-90 rifle, his pocketbook that held a .38-caliber Colt, some books he had bought at a store once we arrived in town, the window with the shades drawn by Buckskin, at my stockings and shoes, and then back at Buckskin.

"There ain't nobody in here but us," I informed him.

Which he clearly knew himself 'cause Waddell, having the day off, said he was going to find a . . . well, that was Waddell's personal business and you don't need to know what he was seeking. Learnt later he found what he was looking for, and he found something else, since he had to see a doc about that when we reached Dodge City.

McConnell had gone with him 'cause he said he'd like to see what a town like Chanute had for harlots, which is why Buckskin and me was alone in our room.

"You don't want to get caught," Buckskin said.

I thought about coming back with *I think you're the one who don't want to get caught.* Wish I had 'cause I don't usually think up replies that fast, but I just parted my lips, then closed them, and that's when Buckskin asked: "You ever treaded the boards?"

"My pa worked for a railroad. He weren't no carpenter."

Chuckling, Buckskin shook his head. "You're a wonder, kid." Then he told me that he once dreamed of being a thespian, which he knew I wouldn't understand. So he told me what a thespian was, and that's how come he knew about *Romeo and Juliet*—which we went to last month as I think I've already mentioned whilst waiting for the trial. He told me he even rode around with a troupe for a time but left it in St. Joe. And that's when I figured out what we—I mean, he—had been doing on Perley's hill back in Emporia. Spying on the Normal girls, but not out of prurient—another one of Buckskin's hifalutin words—desires but to learn more about how to act whilst pretending to be a Bloomer Girl.

Anyhow, that's what we mostly did before

the game. And then we played the game. As a team we stunk. After, we all rode over to the Harvey House to eat supper and wait for the next Atchison, Topeka, and Santa Fe train to take us to wherever it was we was supposed to be going. The reason I can't remember where is 'cause Ruth Eagan come over and sat down where Buckskin and me was wolfing down steaks and corn and drinking our coffee and she says: "It's time."

Buckskin—well, I guess he'd actually be Dolly Madison seeing as how he still wore his Bloomer Girls' uniform—nodded, and he pulled out some money from his pocketbook and laid it on the table. He wiped his mouth daintily with a napkin, and then checked his fingernails the way a gal is supposed to do. When Ruth stood, so did Buckskin and he told me to come along. I paid for my meal and grabbed my bag that held my bat and glove. Buckskin had his bag which held his arsenal of baseball bats and gloves as well as his dangersome firearms. I stood and followed Ruth right along with Buckskin, trying to figure out what she meant when she'd told us that it was time since I knew the train wasn't due for another two hours.

Ruth led the way. We walked out of the eating place and found the stairs and went up them to the second floor of the fancy building which is where the Santa Fe's Kansas Division was headquartered. But there weren't no railroaders in that room. Only Bloomer Girls.

"Sorry we're late," Ruth said happily, "Mother." That last word came out like she was cussing, but she wouldn't say no dirty word 'cause Ruth Eagan is not only pretty, but a real lady, and I knew she was explaining that she was late—for what, I didn't know—on account that her ma had made it happen.

Then Maggie Casey stood, and Maggie wasn't no lady at all, for I'd heard her cuss aplenty on the baseball fields, usually playing in right field while I'd be playing mostly on second base. But I'd been pitching on this day 'cause Russ "Lady" Waddell had asked to rest his arm, but it wasn't his arm that needed resting, it was his head, though he had had to use that arm to drink all that forty-rod the night before which had caused the grief in his noggin this day. So from my position as pitcher, I'd been able to hear some of the things Maggie Casey had called the Chanute ballists.

They weren't pleasant words.

Maggie glared like a mad dog at me and Buckskin, pointed her finger at us, and said: "What are you two doing here?"

Iffen you hang around baseball teams long enough, you learn something about right fielders. They ain't real smart. 'Cause you ain't gotta have much of a brain to play right field. All you need is an arm that's strong enough to break a baseball bat in half and throw a ball something like a tenth of a mile in the air, real, real hard. Maggie Casey could do that. During our game that day she had drilled a Santa Fe brakeman right in his ribs as he was trying to score on a fly he had lofted to the canvas fence. Knocked the wind out of him, it did, meaning Maggie's thrown ball, and that allowed Nelse "Nellie" McConnell to run over and pick up the ball and tag the wheezing brakeman out. At that, some peace officers come out of the stands and lifted the brakeman up, who screamed that two or three ribs of his had been busted and please, God, don't let them puncture his lungs. They carted him out of our makeshift baseball park and it took a long time before the manager of the town-ball team could find a volunteer to replace the brakeman. He finally did, only that fellow struck out in his two at-bats and seemed relieved about it.

"I invited them, Maggie," Ruth said.

"You invited them?" I ain't sure which of those words Maggie Casey emphasized most. Come close to being a three-way tie.

Agnes McGuire, who played a decent second base when Mr. Norris didn't make her sell programs or collect tickets, reached up and tried to grab Maggie's shirt sleeve to give it a gentle tug in a peacekeeping way—'cause second-baggers, me included, is usually trying to keep the peace in one way or another. Maggie slapped Agnes's hand, and Agnes, well, she got her hand out of the vicinity of Maggie's big hams and decided to forget about keeping peace in the meeting room.

"They ain't welcome here," Maggie said to us, and then to other Bloomers: "They wasn't invited."

Now I was ready to turn around and let these Bloomer Girls have their meeting, 'cause I don't like to be where I ain't wanted. Besides, I had left some meat on the bone of my steak, and since I knew all the Bloomer Girls were up here having their secret meeting none of them would even notice me gnawing meat off the bone like a fellow would.

As I was about to turn and leave, Pearl Murphy said: "Ruth invited them. That means they're welcome."

Pearl played left field. She could run fast. Not as fast as me, but I wouldn't bet ag'in' her iffen she was in a forty-yard sprint against McConnell, but, of course, you could time McConnell on a forty-yard run with a calendar. Still, I wouldn't have bet ag'in' Pearl iffen you put McConnell on a quarter-horse and give him a ten-foot lead. Pearl wasn't no bad ballist, neither. She was sort of attractive, too, but nowhere near as sweet-looking as Ruth Eagan in spite of her long limbs, which helped her run fast.

Pearl's comment started quite a commotion. Meaning what Pearl Murphy had just said in the offices of the Santa Fe's Kansas Division, and not when she chased down a fly ball in left field, although, I recollect hearing whistles from men in the stands whilst she was doing that back when we played that game in Fort Scott. The whistles were coming from the spectators that day, as I recall. Russ Waddell, who had been hurling, was whistling, too, till Buckskin told him to knock it off.

But what Pearl said, about us being welcome here since Ruth had invited us, got everyone talking all at once. Except me and Buckskin. Buckskin was getting his carrying bag adjusted so it didn't feel so heavy. Knowing that a Winchester .45-90 must weigh nigh a ton considering how heavy a box of .45-90 shells weighed, I wasn't certain he could make that bag feel no lighter.

I started to turn, ready to bolt to the door so I could escape before things got ugly when Ruth whispered: "No." I straightened in my seat and tried to listen to what was being said even though everyone was talking real fast and real loud at the same time.

I glanced at Katie Maloney who was shaking her head. She started looking at her fingernails, and, dang it all, if she didn't look at 'em just how Buckskin had said women study their nails. She was our starting center fielder, and whilst she had dropped a routine fly ball during our game that afternoon, that didn't happen too often with her. But today it had worked Mr. Norris into what Ruth Eagan called a hissy fit. Buckskin had tried to tell Mr. Norris that it could happen to anyone, that nobody was perfect, which only made our manager angrier, and he quickly pointed out that nobody on his team was even in the vicinity of perfect.

Now everyone in the room was going at it, pointing fingers and making what most folks where I come from would call obscene gestures and using impolite language—and, mind you, I come from a railroad town. It looked like Maggie Casey might come to blows with Maud Nelson, but I wasn't clear on what Maud called Maggie 'cause you really couldn't understand nothing being said by that time. The only woman keeping quiet was Carrie Cassady, who was so timid and quiet that Mr. Norris kept her on the bench during most games. He complained that he couldn't even use her to hawk programs or sell things 'cause she never said anything above a whisper. Buckskin said Carrie come from Salem, Ohio, which, he said, explained her shyness.

A bushel of worry come over me, and I turned to Buckskin to say that we ought to do something before the Chanute constabularies come to arrest us for disturbing the peace, which would make

Mr. Norris even more contrary. Imagine what would happen if we were in the calaboose and couldn't make it to next ball game.

Then there come an explosion like nothing I'd ever heard before.

CHAPTER NINE

. . . There was a couple of small casualties during the game. Ben Underwood, while at the bat, was hit in the face by a ball and incapacitated for a little while, and Walter Duree was felled by a hard blow from a ball on the back of the head, while running from third to home.

The Perry Mirror
Perry, Kansas
May 31, 1906

Ruth Eagan had opened the door and then slammed it shut so hard that the glass window in the top part of that door shattered. Then she had thrown her purse across the room and it hit the far wall. The slamming of the door sounded how I imagined a .45-90 Winchester would roar, till I actually heard one of them rifles sound off. Her purse had made a loud enough noise, too. Things got real quiet after Ruth did those things.

That ain't quite right, neither, but I'm too tired to rip up this page and start all over again. You see, after Ruth's purse hit the wall, and the noise stopped echoing around in that cavernous room, it didn't stay quiet 'cause Ruth Eagan then cut loose with some foul language that made me turn and stare at her. My ears reddened.

Ruth seen me and said: "What the . . . ?" Well, perhaps I should not say what she said to me.

I took a few steps back, careful not to step on no busted glass, then stood in pure shock as Ruth called her teammates some awful names, even if nobody associated with the Kansas City Bloomer Girls would have denied that Maggie Casey wasn't what Ruth said she was. Ruth went right on, saying they—meaning her teammates—had been making such a fuss that it was a wonder the law hadn't come up here, and that if somebody found out that we were holding a meeting in that there office, that we'd likely all land in jail 'cause she had warned Sue Malarkey that folks in this part of the country don't like people using a knife to pick a lock.

Carrie Cassady pointed out: "People are trying to eat their supper downstairs."

It being so quiet after Ruth quit her tirade, we all heard Carrie so clear you'd never know she was almost whispering.

Ruth, she didn't look happy at all, on account that she wasn't. She sucked in a deep breath, let it out, and turned toward me and Buckskin.

"I'm sorry to have inconvenienced you." Her

voice sounded hoarse, but considering how she'd been yelling, 'tweren't no surprise. "Perhaps you should leave us alone as we get a few things straight here," she suggested. By the time she'd put a period to that sentence, Ruth wasn't looking at me and Buckskin no more. She was giving Maggie Casey a stare that brung to mind some faces I'd seen the Widow Amy DeFee give folks after they'd, in her villainous opinion, had slighted her. Made me feel kinda sick to my gut, comparing sweet Ruth Eagan to that vile, evil woman. "But they will be at our next meeting, and they will be welcomed," Ruth said as we headed out.

Buckskin's shoes crunched on the glass and the door squeaked as we slipped into the hallway. It was a miracle the door hadn't come off its hinges in its opening and closing. Buckskin told me to just keep moving as he headed down the stairs and out of the Harvey House that was still filled with people eating. As I glanced inside, I saw a boy who couldn't have been no older than ten. He was grinning 'cause most likely he had heard all kinds of words boys aren't supposed to hear while eating supper and waiting to catch a train, which, I prayed, wouldn't be the train we had to catch.

"What was that all about?" I asked Buckskin later that night.

We was in our sleeping quarters, above Waddell and McConnell, as the train rolled down the Santa Fe tracks.

"Go to sleep," was Buckskin's answer.

"I can't sleep," I told him, but about thirty seconds later, all that *go-to-sleeping* rhythm of the iron wheels knocked me out. I didn't wake up till Buckskin nudged me and told me to hand him the chamber pot, which I did, but didn't like doing it none.

We made it through more forgettable games, Kansas towns all looking the same, but we still weren't nowhere near as far from the Widow Amy DeFee and Judge Brett as I wanted us to be. In fact, we appeared to be inching way too close to Pleasanton for comfort. Of course, the whole state of Kansas was too close to them murdering fiends to make me feel safe.

"I don't believe it," Russ Waddell muttered when we got to the edge of the Perry depot.

I saw that across the street, a bunch of women were busy wrecking a business, armed with axes and hammers and farm tools. They were pounding on the timbers, smashing glass, and wrecking merchandise. I tilted my head to read the name of the business, since they'd already knocked the sign down partway. It read: **Grinter's Soda Fountain.** A group of policemen stood nearby, holding their night sticks but doing nothing to stop the women from destroying bottles of soda pop while knocking the tar out of the soda fountain, the chairs and tables, and just about everything in sight.

Nelse McConnell spat tobacco juice onto a bug. "They swing pretty good," he told Mr. Norris. "You might consider signing them. They look better than some of the petticoats we got playing with us." He didn't say *petticoats*.

Buckskin told McConnell: "Best keep your mouth shut, Nellie."

I knew why McConnell sounded so perturbed. We hadn't been playing worth a fip, but Buckskin kept saying that baseball was like life. You got your ups. And you got your downs. And you just need to ride through the bad times with your head up and your back straight.

Katie Maloney come up beside me and said: "What's going on?"

It looked obvious to me that these women had some sorta grudge against the soda fountain. Nearby, a fellow in a Homburg hat and a plaid sack suit was scribbling page after page in his note pad.

He glanced up and said: "They're enforcing prohibition."

"The dickens you say," said Maggie Casey, or words to that effect, Maggie having come up to the edge of the platform, too.

The gent stopped taking notes long enough to

say that he wrote for the *Mirror*, and that with Governor Hoch and Jackson, whoever he was (I learnt later that he was the state's attorney general, and it was a good thing to know that when I bring back the Widow Amy DeFee later into this narrative), were cleaning up Perry.

"It's been the law of the land across Kansas for better than twenty-five years," the reporter said.

"I've never had a problem getting a shot of rye before," Mr. Norris let him know.

"Civilization," the reporter said. "The corn cribs and the hog pens went first here in Perry. We've put down sandstone at our street crossings, drained the mud holes. What the flood three years back didn't clean up, we're doing ourselves."

While the reporter was saying this them women brung out boxes of bottles and then they started flinging them bottles back inside through the windows they'd already busted. You could hear them breaking on the floor and against the walls and busted-up soda fountain. Some fellows, standing on the street, watching, looked like their best friend had up and died.

"Civilization," Mr. Norris lamented, "can be a sorry thing." He used a different word than *sorry*.

"Town's booming," the reporter said. "We've got our own telephone company now, have moved the stockyards to the east side of town, and we even had a fire engine, but it got burned up three

105

months back when Sallie's restaurant caught fire. The fire station was next door."

He turned away from the ruction across the street and stuck his pencil over his left ear. "Hey, are you all the Bloomer Girls?" He didn't wait for us to answer. "I'd be delighted to get an interview."

Nelse McConnell lifted his voice so that he sounded like some silly girl. "My throat's so dry, I'm not sure I could say more than two words."

The reporter grinned. "Lady, Kansas might have outlawed ardent spirits in the previous century, but the day you find a newspaper office without John Barleycorn is the day there isn't one single newspaper left in America." He closed his pad, which he shoved inside a coat pocket, tipped his hat, and nodded down the street, away from what once had been a saloon that pretended to sell soda pops. Mr. Norris, Russ Waddell, and Nelse McConnell followed the reporter.

Buckskin and me walked to the intersection, where we crossed the street on them flat stones all laid down 'cause Perry had civilized itself.

"There's the hotel," Buckskin said.

Once the ball game commenced, I don't think *civilization* described the town of Perry. At least three hundred Perry folks come to the game on account that just about all the town's businesses closed their doors to watch us play, including that elevator place, the lumberyard, and the hardware store.

The first disagreement come over a song. Perry, or rather, Stone Elevator, prided itself on its band, and since that company brought a lot of money to the city, the umpire—a Mason named Robbins—said it was all right for them to play a tune before we started playing baseball.

A white-bearded man wearing his Union hat and a moth-eaten Army blouse demanded that they play that song some gent named Key wrote during some fight in some war nobody had heard of that was called "The Star-Spangled Banner." He got told that nobody knew that song, and the old man said that, by Jehovah, he knew it and it was appropriate that it be played on this day 'cause when he was preserving the Union they played it before a baseball game at the Union Grounds in Brooklyn, New York, and that that had happened on the 15th of May in the year of our Lord 1862. But someone hollered right back at him that today was the 29th of May and he was two weeks too late to have that tune played.

Someone else put in their two cents, saying that "You're a Grand Old Flag" was a good song that he had heard in some play called *George Washington Jr.* Another gent laughed and opined "Dixie" was a good song. That didn't go over good at all, what with the speaker being a worker at the stockyards and a Texan to boot whilst most of Perry's players come from the railroad or Knapp's sawmill and remained ardent Unionists, like most folks in Kansas.

I recalled in the midst of this that the Gem City Quartet had sung real fine before one of our games, though I couldn't recollect which game or where it was or even what they sang. Finally someone shouted that they might as well play some funeral dirge since there wasn't nothing left of Grinter's Soda Fountain and there wouldn't be nothing left of Perry, Kansas, before the year was out. By that time, the band had started performing, but you couldn't really hear nothing over the police whistles as those coppers who hadn't done nothing to stop the destruction of a private business was doing all they could to keep that Texan from getting murdered.

The various ructions delayed the start of our baseball game twenty-nine minutes.

Perry scored two runs in the first inning, which didn't make Lady Waddell happy 'cause the runs shouldn't have scored. They wouldn't have if Agnes McGuire hadn't let a ball pass through her limbs, or Jessie Dailey—who was playing first base on account Ruth was selling programs— hadn't dropped the ball I threw her from second. Once she picked up the ball, she saw the runner rounding second and moving toward third, so she proceeded to throw it over the canvas fence our crew had erected.

Katie Maloney cut that two-run deficit in half in the bottom of the second inning, when she singled up the middle—"There are a lot of hits up the middle," Buckskin told me—and that hit scored Jessie Dailey who felt that she'd made up for her error in the first inning by scoring a run after she had walked.

Lady Waddell found his fastball and his shine ball—and we took some of the starch out of Perry's ballists when Waddell put a fastball in some guy's jaw, and then Buckskin, playing third, drilled some poor sucker in the back of his noggin while he was trying to score. Anyhow, Perry didn't score again till the fifth inning, but that was on account that this sawmill fellow hit a really good pitch that scored this real tiny Union Pacific guy who wasn't no taller than five-foot, which made it hard to pitch strikes to him. He walked, and that left Waddell complaining that there was no way a fellow that short worked for no railroad 'cause the U.P. don't hire midgets.

Pearl Murphy scored in the bottom of the inning on Katie Maloney's double down the first-base line. We were all excited 'cause we were playing good ball and had forgot all about that first-inning error.

That excitement ended in the top of the sixth inning when Perry scored four runs. Mr. Norris decided that Lady Waddell, who had started out real sharp, wasn't up to snuff, which might have been on account that he had consumed quite a lot of that *Mirror* reporter's rye in the newspaper's office, which had finally caught up with him. Mr. Norris asked me to pitch, but Carrie Cassady wanted to pitch, and Maggie Casey and some other Bloomer Girls said that was the way things were going to be. Now Carrie was a right-hander and didn't have near the speed or curveball of Lady Waddell, even drunk, but Carrie kept the Perry boys off balance and they couldn't do nothing at the plate.

We scored two runs in the bottom of the eighth inning, and had the bases loaded with nary an out, and that's when things got real ugly 'cause the men—and even a few ladies—of Perry didn't agree with the calls made by the umpire, that Mason named Robbins.

There is a rule—Buckskin showed it to me 'cause he had the most current volume there is of the *Constituton and Playing Rules of the National League*—that says, and I copy as best I can: **Under no circumstances shall a captain or player dispute the accuracy of the umpire's judgment and decision on a play.**

Perry's ballists didn't pay that rule no mind, but Buckskin told me that Perry ain't exactly in the National League. Neither is the National Bloomer Girls.

There's really no point for you to hear all them gory details about what happened. We lost, 7-to-4, but that's on account that a fellow from that elevator place took over the umpiring duties since Mr. Robbins couldn't do nothing other than whimper, bleed, and drool.

When we were on the train, Buckskin quoted: " 'The umpire's first decision was usually his last; they broke him in two with a bat, and his friends toted him home on a shutter. When it was noticed that no umpire ever survived a game, umpiring got to be unpopular.' "

Mr. Norris asked what the Sam Hill was that all about, and Buckskin said it was from the Bessemers' game against the Ulsters. Ed Norris swore and went to find the smoking car on the train. Buckskin winked at me and said that I ought to read Mark Twain's *A Connecticut Yankee in King Arthur's Court*, but he gave me *Tom Sawyer* instead.

Still, I reckon it was Nelse McConnell who figured out what had happened at Perry better than anybody else.

"This is what happens when you outlaw liquor."

CHAPTER TEN

Neodesha Sun: The Bloomer aggregation consisted of fourteen persons, eight women and six men. Three or four of the women played ball. The little girl who played first base, whom most of the spectators thought was a boy, is only about 14 years old. Her mother is along with her. They stopped at the Commercial hotel and the landlord says they were an unusually clean and orderly lot. The manager refused to let any of the girls leave the hotel after dark and saw that all retired early.

The Evening Star
Independence, Kansas
June 1, 1906

Reporters. What do they know? The *Sun* wrote that us Bloomer Girls played six men when there weren't more than four, though some folks often mistook Maggie Casey for a guy, and Katie Maloney, too, every now and then. But that ink-slinger got his facts right about that manager at the Commercial. Fool wouldn't let nobody upstairs after we got checked in, but Russ Waddell and Nelse McConnell got out, dressed in their men duds, by going down the back staircase, and that proved to be their mistake. 'Cause when they tried to come back in after midnight, the back door was locked and two policemen guarded the outside staircase. The old boy at the front desk remained awake, protecting all the girls upstairs, and he told Waddell and McConnell that they weren't registered guests and had best skedaddle. Since he, the hotel manager, held a cannon of a shotgun, Waddell and McConnell left. Considering the hay on their clothes, me and Buckskin figured they'd slept in a livery, which is why Buckskin sent me back up to our room to fetch the grips of our two bunkmates, and then Waddell and McConnell had to find somewhere to get dressed in their uniforms and look like girls and not saddle tramps who'd just spent the night with horses, donkeys, and mules 'cause we had to catch the first train out and play a game that Thursday in Independence.

We were down in the southern part of the state for a while, not that far from Coffeyville, when Buckskin told us all about how the Dalton boys got shot to hell and gone back in '92 whilst they tried to rob two banks in one day.

"Daltons," Waddell said with a snort. "Not an honest bunch in the whole family."

Buckskin shook his head. "You're wrong there, Russ. Frank was the best of the bunch. Good man. Honest. About as fine a man as I ever met. Deputy marshal for Judge Parker's court. Got gunned down by a whiskey-runner in 'Eighty-Seven. But as far as Frank's brothers . . . Bob, Grat, Emmett . . . yeah, I guess you're likely right."

"I don't know those Daltons," Waddell said. "I'm talking about Courtney and Reed Dalton. Umpired in the Western League in 'Ninety-Nine. The Bisons and Hoosiers must have paid them aplenty, considering the calls they made. My grandma could've umped better than those two idiots, even after that bad whiskey left her blind."

That got me to thinking, not about blind grandmas or outlaws or how Buckskin Compton might have known a deputy marshal who got killed almost twenty years earlier, but that we was in Independence which wasn't far from Coffeyville which wasn't too far from Pleasanton and the Widow Amy DeFee and her man-killing judge unless they had lit a shuck for Mexico and I was playing baseball dressed like a gal for nothing. And then I found the itinerary for the next week or two that Mr. Norris had give us that noted all the towns where we'd be staying and the names of the hotels and what time the games were and when we'd be leaving for the next place.

I learnt we weren't never getting out of eastern Kansas no time soon.

Anyhow, we boarded the morning's Missouri Pacific train and rode straight south down to Independence. I sat alone since we weren't going no more than fifteen miles, and Buckskin went with McConnell and Waddell to the smoking car. I practiced looking at my fingernails the way Buckskin said I was supposed to, and then somebody cleared her throat and said: "Lucy, do you mind if I sit down?" I stopped looking at my nails, including the split one on my pointer finger that I got trying to field a bad hopper that danged near drove that tip down two joints. My mouth dropped open 'cause standing right next to me was Ruth Eagan.

Girl's voice. Girl's voice. Girl's voice.

That run through my mind, but first I looked away from Ruth Eagan, which allowed me to close my mouth. I saw Mrs. Eagan sitting up about four rows and frowning while pretending to be listening to Gypsie O'Hearn talk about how Dr. Rose's Improved Kidney and Liver Cure, which she got through Sears, Roebuck & Co., for only eighty-five cents, had worked a wonder on her dysmenorrhea. 'Cause you couldn't look at Mrs. Eagan too long without turning to stone, I whipped my head back to sweet, pretty Ruth Eagan and said: "Sure."

A half minute later I remembered to slide over

and move Buckskin's heavy bat bag—made heavier on account of the arsenal he carried—off the opposite seat so that Ruth could sit down.

"I'm sorry," she said once she had settled herself into the seat.

I wet my lips and hid my fingernails, trying to give her an ordinary look whilst trying to figure out what she could be apologizing for. It couldn't have been for all them filthy words she had cut loose with back when we had had that meeting upstairs of the Harvey House 'cause she surely must have heard me cut loose a couple of times when she was playing first base after that ball had bounced off a stone and slammed into the finger on my throwing hand and not into my baseball glove.

"You were right," she said, and let out the longest sigh.

I sat up a little straighter 'cause *you were right* ain't a sentence I hear every day.

"When you told me I shouldn't play first base wearing a catcher's mitt," Ruth explained.

"Oh," said I. First, I thought if that were the case then why had she played first base today wearing that big old mitt, but I knew not to say that 'cause that would make me a louse, which is what Buckskin said I was after I'd told Ruth that she'd never play baseball as well as a man as long as she used that mitt anywhere except behind the plate. I didn't want to be no louse never again.

The railroad-car door opened and a man in a brown suit hurried down the aisle.

"Listen," I said. "The rules say you can wear any glove, any mitt, any size, if you're playing first base or catcher. I just don't see many men doing that. The rules say other fielders have to use a glove like mine."

She smiled. "No more than ten ounces. Not more than fourteen inches around the palm."

That impressed me. The only reason I knew the rule about catchers and first basemen was 'cause Buckskin let me know the facts all them days ago after I'd made Ruth unhappy and Buckskin had called me a louse.

"Ruth," I said, and leaned kinda close to her, so that I could smell her, but then I rammed my spine against the back of that hard-rock seat and made sure I couldn't smell her lilac and lemon scent no more, and I said: "Spalding is making mitts for first basemen. And basewomen. Ummm. Waddell. Lady Waddell, I mean, she's got one that she uses when she ain't pitching. But you couldn't use hers. I mean, she's a lefty and you ain't," though I'd heard some coaches say they wanted lefties playing first base.

Had to get my breathing, brain, and tongue working properly again. "They're not as big as a catcher's mitt. The first baseman's mitt, I mean. But they're bigger than mine. Well-padded, too. 'Specially around the wrist and thumb. For them

117

bad hops thrown far 'cross the field. I mean, I wouldn't want to take a throw from Buck- . . . Dolly Madison as hard as . . . she . . . throws from third to first."

Ruth smiled. "Dolly's throws sting my hand when I'm wearing my catcher's mitt. Anyway, I wanted you to know I've ordered a new glove. Well, Mother did. It should reach us in Axtell."

I got inspired and showed her my purple finger. "I could've used it yesterday."

She laughed. "But that's your throwing hand."

"Still could have used it."

Her laugh got harder, and I felt about as comfortable as I'd ever felt talking to a pretty girl whilst I was dressed up like a National Bloomer Girl. There we sat, making jokes and laughing and feeling real good, and even though trains practically always put me to sleep, I felt perky and wide awake and about as happy as a guy can feel when he's dressed in a girl's uniform and hiding from an evil woman and her crooked judge friend who'd done made me an orphan. But living your life can be like playing a baseball game. One inning you think you're a king 'cause you just sent a screaming fastball between the center and right fielders and wound up on second base clapping your hands and hearing the crowd booing 'cause your hit just tied the score. Two innings later, you're trying to shake the feeling back into a finger that might be broke and the

118

crowd is hooting and making fun of you and even your own mean center fielder is yelling that you ain't worth a hoot. (It's a proved fact that outfielders don't know what it's like to try to field a sharp ground ball that hits a stone and takes a path that not even Nap Lajoie could have anticipated even before he got spiked so bad last year that the doctors feared they might have to saw off his limb.)

Ruth's smile got turned into a frown, because she saw me frowning, which I was doing as I watched Mrs. Eagan making her way down the aisle, followed by the fellow who'd come in the car wearing the brown suit. Right soon, Ruth's ma stood above us and she didn't even give me a mean look, just said to Ruth: "Come along, child. This handsome gentleman with *The Sporting News* has requested an interview with you."

That handsome gentleman removed his hat and bowed at Ruth and said: "Louis Friedman. Special correspondent, Miss Eagan. Out of Topeka."

"He writes for *Variety*, too," Mrs. Eagan said. "Remember . . . I'll tell you what to say."

I studied that dark-haired fellow with a thin, waxed mustache and a gleam in his eye and his hair all perfect and shining and smelling like Old Reliable Hair and Whisker Dye, the scent of which I remembered all too well from that time when Pa come across about a dozen bottles inside

119

a box some drummer had left behind at the depot and proceeded to drink them empty.

Ruth didn't look too happy, though I would've been thrilled to get asked to talk to a reporter from that sporting journal, even if he was only a correspondent who used too much hair oil that made me sick to my stomach. I had to move my legs out of Ruth's way so *The Sporting News* could make her famous. As Ruth walked back down the aisle, Mrs. Eagan give me a look that wasn't that far from the faces on them folks from Perry after they practically drawed and quartered the umpire. Louis Friedman hadn't even bothered to introduce hisself to me or even give me a by-his-leave before he walked back to the front of the coach.

I'm sure my face didn't look no better when Gypsie O'Hearn slid into the seat across from me that had, in my mind, been the throne of Queen Ruth Eagan. Gypsie waited till Mrs. Eagan got back into her seat with her daughter and the nice-looking *Sporting News* gent, before leaning closer to me and saying: "How 'bout you, hon? Do you take Doctor Rose's Improved Kidney and Liver Cure when the dysmenorrhea strikes you each month? Or do you just grin, bleed, and bear it?"

Tilting her head back, she laughed, like a hydrophoby coyote, and asked if she could get a cigarette off me. Ready made. She didn't like to roll her own. Richmond Straight Cut No. 1s, preferably, but any kind would do.

"I don't smoke," I told her.

"Didn't ask if you smoked," she said. "I asked you if you had a cigarette?" She added some salty words to describe the cigarette she wanted. After which she laughed and put up her limbs, straddling my legs, asking if I'd rub her feet 'cause they ached. Next, she asked me where I was sleeping when we rode out of Independence and if I'd like some company. Then she kind of puffed herself up so that her Bloomer Girls' blouse got sort of bigger. That horrible laugh of hers come again when my ears got red, but she wouldn't move her legs. We hadn't gone but maybe four or five miles, which meant I had to ride all that rest of the way held prisoner by Gypsie O'Hearn's limbs.

CHAPTER ELEVEN

When the dainty bloomer lassies
  come to town,
Wearing costumes suited to the
  circus clowns,
There will be a lot of people
Climbing house-top and church
  steeple
Just to get a better chance to
  peep aroun'.
When the dainty bloomer lassies
  come to town,
Plump as quails, with sparkling
  eyes and faces brown,
There will be an awful flurry
And the boys will have to hurry
For their places on the
  bleachers close, low down. . . .
                    The Oskaloosa Times
                    Oskaloosa, Kansas,
                    May 24, 1906

We made it as far north as Oskaloosa, which is between Kansas City and Topeka and a bit north, but is on the Atchison, Topeka, and Santa Fe. I thought about leaving my teammates and buying a ticket that would take me to wherever the Santa Fe line went west. I might have done that except that would have meant I'd never see Ruth again. Besides, for all I knew, the Widow Amy DeFee could've been hiding out in Santa Fe or anywhere else I got off the train. On top of all that, I knew our next ball games were to be played in Holton and Concordia—they were west, so maybe we'd finally start putting some miles between me and the widow and her judge. But then I imagined her showing up at one of our games with her 30.-30. Being on the dodge, I tell you, doesn't get you nothing but worries and a sick feeling in your gut.

Those Oskaloosans knew how to play base-ball better than some of the town teams we'd seen, which come as a surprise 'cause I didn't think men who worked in factories that made bridle bits and ice—not at the same factory, mind you, the bridle bit building being in the center of town whilst the ice got made somewhere down Big Slough Creek, wherever that was—could play ball. Anyhow, it was a good game, with about fifty men and women and kids of color in attendance, and they cheered us and the Oskaloosans. The umpire come from the electric light plant and was an Episcopal, but he called a game better than them Daltons of the old Western League, according to Waddell. Waddell didn't even give the parson one ugly look, and McConnell only cussed underneath his breath sixty or seventy times.

After the game, we went to get something to eat, though we were taking the 7:45 to Concordia on the Missouri Pacific, not the Santa Fe. There, Ruth come up to us and told Buckskin and me to follow her, so we did. We waited out on the porch for a while before a Negress come along and said that we should follow her, so we did, Buckskin toting his bag and me hauling mine, a few blocks to the Baptist church for the colored folks.

The Negress opened the door and told us to take any seat, which we done on the back pew. I was surprised to find Jessie Dailey, Maude Sullivan, and Agnes McGuire already there. Not much time passed before Pearl Murphy come in with Katie Maloney. Then Carrie Cassidy and Maggie Casey walked through them doors, and after that the rest of the Bloomer Girls come inside, excepting Gypsie O'Hearn, who Maggie said wouldn't be with us this evening on account she got in her cups and was sicker than a dog, which was fine with me because I still felt mighty uncomfortable around her after that train ride down to Independence where she had trapped me in my seat with her limbs.

Normally, folks talk in hushed voices before church services begin, but nobody in our group was whispering. And there wasn't nobody in the church excepting the Bloomer Girls, plus Buckskin and me. (Buckskin has been scolding

124

me that I really ought to say *Buckskin and me* and not *me and Buckskin* 'cause the former is correct English and makes me sound learnt instead of ignorant. He went on to say there were a few more things he ought to point out about how I write and how I talk, allowing that a boy has to learn to walk before he can run and then must master the running part before he can ride a bicycle. I told him that he knew I could run because I played second base and had stole eight bases without being thrown out yet, and he knew I could ride a bicycle because he had seen my Hawthorne. He told me to shut up and just write the best I can.)

At length, Pearl Murphy stood up and moved out into the center aisle so she could see all of us. She said: "I guess we might as well call this meeting to order."

That made me feel more comfortable 'cause it looked like Pearl Murphy would be running this show, and not Maggie Casey, so the chances of me not getting cussed at or having my eyeballs scratched out seemed much improved. I didn't know there was gonna be no meeting when I'd followed Ruth, though I figured that Buckskin must've knew, only he didn't tell me nothing because he likely expected that I wouldn't have come had I known there was going to be a meeting, and I expect that he was right in that mind of thinking.

"First," Pearl Murphy said, "I'd like to thank Buckskin Compton and . . ."

My mouth dropped open, my heart stopped beating, and I felt plumb horrified. She hadn't called Buckskin by his Bloomer Girls' name but by Buckskin Compton. Worser, she hadn't said I was Lucy Totton but called me by my whole name, even used my middle name, which nobody should have knew excepting for Mr. Norris as that's what I'd written down on my contract. I all but died of shame and terror, the shame being that some of the girl players who was sitting on the aisles in front of us turned and stared at us, but mostly me. The terror being that Mr. Norris and Mrs. Eagan might rip up my contract and put me out in the streets of Oskaloosa, which wasn't far enough away from Pleasanton being right smack in eastern Kansas. Then I might face instant and painful death from the hands or rifle of the Widow Amy DeFee.

Pearl Murphy hadn't said nothing. Nobody else had, neither. So she waited till folks stopped staring at . . . *Buckskin and me* . . . then said: "Does anyone have any objections if I yield the floor to Mister Compton?" She wasn't asking everyone, of course, just Maggie Casey, who didn't say nothing, because Pearl Murphy raised her noggin and smiled at Buckskin and said: "The floor is yours, Billy."

So Buckskin stood, but he didn't step out of the

aisle, only kind of leaned against the edge of the pew, and begun talking, but not until he took off his wig.

"Thank you, Miss Murphy. Thank all of you. So my understanding is that you want to play men's teams."

"We've been playing men," Maggie Casey said without looking at Buckskin. "Or maybe you think Oskaloosa had girls deck out in men's garb and grow beards in today's game."

"What we want, what we need," Agnes McGuire said, "is to play a team of men . . ."

Buckskin grinned and finished the sentence for her. "Without Waddell, McConnell, my young pard here, and me."

"That's the only way we can prove that women are as good as men," Carrie Cassady said as soft as a mouse.

What she said left me surprised. I could expect that kind of thinking from Maggie Casey, but Carrie . . . I mean . . . she hailed from Salem, Ohio, wherever that was.

"Amen, sister," said Katie Maloney, patting Carrie's arm—only Katie Maloney's patting was more like pounding, and Carrie quickly took her arm off the back of the pew and out of range.

"Why do you need to beat a team of men ballists?" Buckskin asked.

"Because this is the Twentieth Century," Maggie said.

I feared things might get out of control, just as they had done back at that Harvey House.

"Don't you think we ought to have the right to play for the Cubs or the White Sox?" Katie Maloney hollered.

"Or even the Boston Americans?" added Sue Malarkey.

"At least we deserve the chance to try out for a professional team," sweet, pretty Ruth Eagan said, but she didn't yell like Maggie, Katie, and Sue had. Nor did she whisper like Carrie.

"Or the Lincoln Ducklings, or some other Western League team. Or even Oskaloosa if we had to live in this sinkhole," said someone whose voice I couldn't recognize and who didn't really say *sinkhole*.

Buckskin hooked his thumb toward the closed door. "The Negroes were kind enough to let you use their house of worship to hold this meeting. How many Negro men do you see playing for the Chicago teams, or even the Boston Americans, or the Lincoln Ducklings, or any professional team?"

"Because . . . ," Maude Sullivan started to say, but didn't finish.

Ruth, though, she said something that Buckskin later defined as profound, telling me to look up that word, *profound,* in the dictionary he'd bought. I picked up my own copy of *Webster's Common School Dictionary* later when we were in Denver.

"There aren't any playing for the Bloomer Girls, either."

Things got quiet, like we was in a church—exactly where we were—but that silence lasted only about five or six seconds.

"Women like us were getting at least a chance ten years ago," Maggie Casey, said, and she was ugly when she was standing. She kind of nudged Pearl Murphy toward the pews on the other side of the aisle. "Lizzie Arlington played for the Reds. The *Cincinnati* Reds. And I bet you and your little puppy dog . . ."—reckon I was the little puppy dog—"sitting there about to wet his britches couldn't hit Lizzie's fastball."

By grab, Buckskin just grinned. "I probably couldn't," he said. "And neither could you. Any of you."

Not grinning, Maggie Casey come down the aisle like Satan had latched upon her soul, and said all sorts of things that one shouldn't never say in public and absolutely never in a church, especially in a church, a Baptist church, in Kansas.

Buckskin, though, he weren't scairt like me, even though his bat bag lay on the floor opposite of me. Maggie Casey looked ready to unleash all of her anger out on him before he could ever get to that rifle, but Buckskin didn't budge an inch.

He said: "Ladies, you couldn't even beat Oskaloosa."

Being the truth, them words must've registered even to Maggie Casey on account that she stopped her charge. The room turned quiet.

Buckskin said: "You want suffrage. You want equality. I understand that. But baseball is a tough sport. Professional baseball is even harder. And you need to face this fact . . . men are stronger than women."

Pearl Murphy said: "Say that after you've pushed a ten-pound baby outta your body through your . . ."

Well, my face turned redder than the Oskaloosas' lace-up shirts or the stripes on their pristine white caps.

Buckskin, he remained unflappable, but when you mostly play third base, you get used to hard shots coming right at you. He said: "I readily admit that this species would have died out thousands of years ago had reproduction been placed upon us."

I didn't figure out what they was talking about till I wrote down these words just now.

The Bloomer Girls hadn't expected that.

"Is this what you want? Really. Deep down in your soul?" Buckskin kept staring right through Maggie Casey, who looked like she didn't know what she should do. "Because the fans aren't going to call you 'New Women' . . . or 'Gibson Girl,' or anything like that. You'll be called freaks. And much, much worse."

He stopped talking, but the church weren't silent long.

Pearl Murphy said: "Maybe at third base, you can't hear what those skinflints who line up beyond the outfield fence call us."

"I'm not deaf," Buckskin said.

"American women were making progress," Maude Sullivan said, "even into the 'Nineties. Then the Twentieth Century rolls around and we're back in the Dark Ages."

"Except in Wyoming," Ruth pointed out.

"Fool Wyoming," Maggie Casey snapped, but, yeah, it wasn't *fool* that she said. "They have to let women vote and hold office because there aren't enough men stupid enough to live in that wind-blown perdition. If women didn't live there, they'd have pronghorns and jack rabbits as mayors and justices."

Ruth's face turned redder than mine had, but now my ears were burning hot, and if Maggie Casey had been a fellow, I'd have punched her in the nose for conversing that way to a sweet girl who could play a decent first base and would keep on playing that way once her new first baseman's mitt showed up in Axtell.

"So what is it that you can do for us, *mister?*" Maggie Casey asked, and the way she said *mister* wasn't what anybody would call respectful.

"I want to coach you," Buckskin said.

"Isn't that what Egg-Head Norris does?" Maud Nelson asked.

"He's a manager," Buckskin said. "A businessman. I can *coach*." He glanced at me. "With my pard here to help out some."

CHAPTER TWELVE

These are no ugly women, but it is safe to say that the Bloomer Girls were less beautiful than any women ever seen in Holton.

The Holton Signal
Holton, Kansas
June 7, 1906

B est put your wig back on," I told Buckskin when he was walking out of the Baptist church where he had spent some private time talking with Pearl, Maggie, and Katie about "things," as he said, whilst I didn't have to take off no wig 'cause I didn't wear one, my hair being so long and so virginal, whatever that means. I leaned against the frame wall of the Baptist church and started thinking that it was a woeful life to be living if I didn't even have to wear no wig to get mistook for a female. Next thing I knew sweet Ruth had come up to me, smiling.

Not smiling like someone had told her a funny joke, but a pleasing, plumb nice smile.

"Good evening," she started, pausing as her smile brightened, then calling me by my rightful name, not Lucy Totton.

I said: "I'm sorry to have frauded you, Miss Ruth."

Cocking her head a mite, pursing them rosy lips, Ruth said: "*Frauded* me?"

My head bobbed, before I recollected to take off my ballcap, which I hadn't taken off whilst inside the church. I thought that God wouldn't be too happy about that, but He likely already felt perturbed from all them Sunday ball games we had taken part in.

"Passing myself off as a Bloomer Girl," I explained.

She grinned again. "I think I'm old enough to know the difference between a nice young man and a woman who plays second base like a man."

My shoulders stopped sagging. She'd called me a man, not a boy.

The wind picked up, not that it wasn't blowing already because the blamed wind never stopped blowing in Kansas, and I tried to think of something sweet and smart to say.

The other Bloomer Girls had all left, so it was me and Ruth who thanked the folks, who were waiting outside, for loaning us their church, and then me and Ruth left. We weren't talking, or holding hands, just walking and enjoying the breeze. Till a gust blew sand in my eyes and took Ruth's baseball cap all the way into the center of a corral outside a livery. I had to go in and fetch it, then we continued on to the Missouri

Pacific depot where we waited for our train.

It took us to Holton, which wasn't but one or two stops to the northwest on the M-P. We all got settled into our hotel easy enough, and went to bed, though I'd slept plenty on the train.

It was a pot-bellied man who called hisself Mayor Kuhn who greeted us before the game as we was climbing into the omnibus to take us from the hotel to the field where our crew had put up the equipment earlier that morning. The mayor proclaimed this to be the greatest event in the history of Holton. He paused angrily when McConnell spit between his teeth at this announcement. Though he wore spectacles thicker than the bottom of a beer bottle, the mayor looked long and hard at McConnell, who had forgotten to shave that morning because Holton, unlike Perry, wasn't right yet upholding the state laws that outlawed liquor. Flustered now, Mayor Kuhn forgot what he was supposed to say next. We waited, getting bored, and at length Mr. Norris thanked the mayor for his generosity and we climbed onto the omnibus. Buckskin, me, and Waddell had to help the still-roostered McConnell get aboard. We took off and got to the field where another person give a talk.

Unlike the mayor, she didn't forget her speech at all—not one word.

"What you women are doing . . . ," she began.

That's when McConnell burped, and I mean he burped so loud that they likely heard him way down in Oskaloosa.

The woman stopped, stared at McConnell, and it wasn't no kind or forgiving stare. It was a look that commanded respect from everyone, even Maggie Casey. Or, as it turned out, Nelse "Nellie" McConnell.

"Beg your pardon," McConnell said before he slumped down onto our bench.

"What you *women* are doing," she said, only this time she nodded at the individual girls, ignoring Buckskin, Mr. Norris, and Waddell, though she did, gosh dang it, nod at me, "is a small but important step on our way to equality."

She introduced herself as Ella Brown, saying she taught at Campbell College, wherever that was, and that for two years *she* had served as the city attorney in Holton, and she meant this here Holton in Kansas and not nowheres up in Wyoming.

"Look around you when you leave our fair city," she said. "Our Hook and Ladder Company has three engines, and our volunteers protect not only the city, but the county. We've taxed dogs since 'Seventy-Two."

That caused Buckskin to lean and whisper: "Do the dogs pay those taxes in dollar bills or dog-goned barks?" But luckily, Miss Ella Brown was still talking so she mustn't have heard Buckskin.

"The sidewalks around the town square, once

plank, are now brick or iron. Plans are in the works for sewers, for drinking fountains on each corner of the square, and to have our houses numbered. But is this progress?"

"No!" the Bloomers bellowed, which caused Mr. Norris to cuss because he messed up the line-up card he was filling out whilst sitting on the bench and cussing the now sleeping McConnell for being a walking whiskey vat.

Ella Brown didn't act like she'd heard that neither, but we all knew she had. Jo-fired she was, and so were our Bloomer Girls. "I," she said, "was the first woman to dare to enter the law department at K.U. in Eighteen Ninety. But that is nothing compared to what you young, strong women are doing. Do you know how long it took the Saint Louis Browns to put even a ladies' toilets in their baseball stadium? Oh, they wanted women to come to their games, thinking it would lessen the hooliganism at those sordid affairs in that detestable beer and whiskey league. So women came to stadiums across our United States, paying twenty-five cents like men, to cheer on the team that represented their city, their town, their league. They called those women krankets. As in *cranks,* for any women who cheered on baseball, surely must be eccentric or just plain mad."

Again, Buckskin leaned over. "She ought to be a preacher," he whispered.

"Oh, it's fine for women to play baseball in college, at Vassar or Mount Holyoke, and, sure, bloomers are great for women if they want to ride a bicycle. *Men* even allowed us to take part in pedestrianism in the 'Seventies. Walking is fitting exercise for this 'fairer sex,' especially, the male organizers said, if they can make all women competitors wear offensive bows and freakish attire. Well, we are not freaks and we walk, we ride bicycles, and if we want to play baseball, we will play baseball because it is our right. This is Nineteen-Aught-Six. Almost forty years ago, Wyoming gave us suffrage, and do you know how many states have followed suit? Three. Three more states . . . Colorado, Utah, and Idaho. Women ballists, we have the National Consumers League, the Woman's Christian Temperance Union, and Women's Trade Union League. And you, the National Bloomer Girls, are the first step to our goal. But our goal is not for a Women's National League of Professional Base Ball Clubs or some Women's American League of Professional Baseball Clubs, but, by thunder, professional, semi-professional, and town-ball clubs that allow women and men to compete together, to compete as a team. We love our sports, and we should be allowed to play them. You are taking our first step to equality. And I dream that one day, I won't hear the ridiculous statement . . . 'May the best *man* win,' but 'May the best *player* win' . . . so . . ."

That's when Buckskin leaned over and whispered: "Better."

Which caused me to miss most of the rest of what the lady lawyer said, not that I was paying that much attention to her anyway, because she was shouting like she was an engineer who spent too much time in a locomotive cab and had gone practically deaf, so if he was deaf, he figured nobody could hear what he was saying, which didn't make no sense, but you couldn't explain that to a deaf engineer. Or this lady lawyer.

Still, I got most of what the lady lawyer said because the reporter for the Horton *Headlight* put it all down in the paper that Buckskin bought a copy of the next morning before we rode the train up to Axtell, which is where I went to the post office with Ruth to fetch her new first basewoman's mitt that had been sent special order from St. Louis.

"What?" I didn't speak in no whisper but shouted it, on account it was the only way Buckskin could hear what I was saying above the commotion them Bloomer Girls and Miss Brown was making, hollering something fierce, stomping their baseball shoes, and banging their bats on the ground.

"Better," Buckskin said. "Not best. Comparatives and superlatives."

"What?" I repeated.

"Better is used when comparing two things. Best is . . ."

"What?"

Buckskin screamed in my ear: "I'll tell you after the game!"

Which the Bloomer Girls won, 14-to-3. Nobody from Horton was happy about that, excepting that lady lawyer, who, all giddy, slapped my shoulder and said I'd done a crackerjack job.

That put me in such a foul mood, that I sulked all that night in the hotel, all through breakfast the next morning, and even more when Buckskin showed me the *Headlight* on the train.

It just ain't right that a fellow my age gets mistaken for a gal. So irritated was I that the rhythm of the train couldn't even help put me to sleep.

Buckskin, seeing I couldn't sleep, nudged me and said: "Let's go."

We went to the smoking car, and Buckskin slid into the seat next to Mr. Norris. I took the seat closest to the window and tried to breathe in air that didn't stink of cigars, pipes, and cigarettes, and closed my eyes so they didn't burn, but that's not to say I wasn't listening to what Buckskin and Mr. Norris were conversing about.

"Our girls played well yesterday," Buckskin said.

"I could have pulled a muffin nine from the charity ward at Saint Joseph's and beaten those

140

losers." Mr. Norris kept playing solitaire using his hard-backed carrying case for a table. I knew this even with my eyes closed 'cause I could hear the slap of the cards.

"They did it without McConnell catching."

"They didn't do it without you catching, Waddell pitching, and the boy at second."

"I thought Carrie did a good job at third."

The slapping noise of the cards stopped.

"They didn't have a batter on the whole team who could figure out Russ's curveball or fastball. That Quaker half-wit fielded two slow rollers. That loud-mouthed, pettifogging petticoat of a solicitor could've done that."

"Those plays aren't easy to make," Buckskin said.

I opened my eyes as Mr. Norris sat up straighter and I watched his reflection in the window. He glanced over at me, but must've thought I was sleeping, which was natural, because that's what I usually do on trains. Then he turned back to Buckskin, leaned forward.

"Picking up a ball off the ground," he said, "and throwing it across the field before a two-hundred-forty-four pound slob or a gimp can run ninety feet when it's ninety-five degrees and the wind's blowing from right field to home plate . . . that's infinitely easier than shooting two men off galloping horses at four hundred yards. Don't you agree, Buck?"

I became pretty interested and curious about the conversation nobody figured I was listening to.

Mr. Norris placed his deck of cards in his coat pocket and pulled out a bottle of whiskey, took a swig, and passed it over to Buckskin.

When Buckskin took a swallow, Mr. Norris leaned in close and brought his voice down to a whisper, but since there wasn't no woman lawyer preaching about suffrage and Susan B. Anthony and Wyoming, and no noise except the typical train noise, which I'd gotten used to with all the traveling, I heard him plain as day.

"I know you love baseball, Buck. And I know you really want to coach and manage a team. But you need to think about yourself. I hired you on to save your life. We get enough press as it is. Do you want to have people take note of you like they do Waddell?" Mr. Norris paused just long enough to take a swig of liquor. "They've got a new prison in Wyoming, Buck, four or five years old now. They'd love to have you making brooms till they could let you test out that Julian Gallows they used on your pal, Tom Horn, three years ago."

Buckskin wasn't saying nothing.

"You never struck me as a fool, Buck. Let the girls take care of themselves. You take care of yourself. I'll take care of the team. Tread lightly, pard."

Wasn't much after that before I really fell sound asleep, and stayed that way till Buckskin woke me to say we was in Axtell. Getting woke up with my head hurting from resting against a train window for a number of hours, I had trouble figuring out if I had dreamt that conversation. But then, like it had been a dream, I plumb forgot all about it for a while.

The Bloomer team arrived in Axtell around 2:30. Mr. Norris had sent the crew on ahead of us to put up our canvas fences and grandstand in Axtell. As we waited at the depot to find out when we needed to be at the ball field and then what time the train would be leaving for Concordia, Ruth came up to me.

She said she couldn't wait to get her new glove, which had been mailed to Axtell, and she asked me to take her to the post office to fetch the package. Carrie Cassady offered to make sure Ruth's luggage was taken care of properly. Since the post office was right across the street, Buckskin told us we'd best hurry before Mrs. Eagan caught sight of us. So we hurried across the street.

CHAPTER THIRTEEN

. . . The "manager" of the alleged "lady" ball team was about the toughest looking specimen of humanity seen in this city for some time. Some of those attending the game say it is not the first time they have been played for suckers, for a number of times last year a gang was picked up some where and run in under some name, and as a result they paid their money to see a rotten game. A Sunday ball game is bad enough, but that such an attraction should be pulled off on a Sunday afternoon within the city limits, is a disgrace to the city and an insult to every respectable lady in the community.

The Brown County World
Hiawatha, Kansas
June 15, 1906

For a small town of maybe seven hundred folks and about seven million flies, Axtell had a gigantic post office. And I sure didn't expect to see so many folks inside.

One gent was trying to cash a money order, whilst another worked one of them telegraph machines. A tired-looking, old fellow was complaining to somebody behind the counter that driving them rural routes had turned into a misery 'cause nobody bothered to drag the roads, while a woman sending some letters nodded like she understood whatever the postal worker was telling her. Weren't long, though, before everybody stopped talking and just stared at Ruth and me, but mostly at sweet, pretty Ruth. A gent behind the head-nodding lady turned around to face us as he must've been sick of hearing the postal carrier complain about roads. He removed his straw hat, bowed, and stepped aside, saying: "You two ladies must be from the National Bloomer Girls."

Ruth, never much of a talker, except when she got mad, especially at Maggie Casey, made her head bob whilst the man was putting his straw hat back atop his bald head. So I said—"Yes, sir,"— in my girl's voice about the same time he give his name, Mr. Sehy, editor and publisher of the *Anchor*, as he produced a notebook and pencil from his pocket. He requested an interview.

The nodding lady, finished with her mailing, smiled at Ruth but she gave me a look that said she might be suspicious of what I was up to, then she was gone. At the same time, the fellow trying to cash the money order turned around and said to no one in particular: "This town has a baseball team?"

When I glanced at him, my heart just about stopped beating, because he weren't no gent at all, but Judge Kevin Brett. I jerked down my cap and turned toward the fellow working the telegraph who stood up suddenly and announced: "That's funny. It just went dead."

To which the old codger who was complaining about the roads sighed and said: "Probably the weight of the flies collapsing the line."

"Our Blues," said the fellow who had just finished counting out the cash for Judge Brett, "will be playing the National Bloomer Girls of Kansas City in less than an hour."

Ruth just smiled, and the judge moved over toward us. I said in my highest and most nervous girl's voice: "Ruth . . . Ruth Eagan . . . here has a baseball glove that was supposed to be delivered to this post office."

Thankfully, the mail clerk called the judge back to the window to get his cash, and then the old guy who didn't like flies and undragged roads, though I don't reckon anybody truly likes flies, said he knew where that package was, and went to the back of the building which was packed high with boxes, crates, and sacks of mail, magazines, and newspapers scattered across the floor.

I strode over to the counter because I wanted to help Ruth, but mostly because that section lay clear on the other side of the room from where that man-killing judge stood getting his money. Much later, I wondered if Widow Amy DeFee and Judge Brett had swindled that money out of the insurance company, or if it was ill-gotten gains they'd stole from other honest folks.

"Baseball," the *Anchor* editor began his interview, "is a dangerous game, Miss Eagan."

Ruth said: "Dangerous?"

The editor said: "Why, yes, I have received reports this very week that a boy in Kansas City, not seventeen years old, was hit over his heart by a pitch and died instantly."

"How horrible and sad," said Ruth, because she was nice and liked people, even ones she'd never met.

The man working the telegraph tapped relentlessly, about as fast as my heart kept pounding, and said: "This is the queerest thing."

Sweating now and thinking my heart might just quit, I asked a man behind the counter: "Should I go help the fellow look for the package, sir?"

But the fellow said: "Ma'am, civilians are not allowed in the mail room." From the corner of my eye, I spied the judge glancing at me, and I lowered my head and muttered: "I understand, sir."

The judge stepped away from the counter, as

the telegrapher said: "It's still not working. I don't understand."

At the same time, Ruth said to the reporter: "Lightning can strike anywhere, Mister Sehy, whether you're playing the game or not."

The judge counted his money and, once satisfied, shoved it in his pocket, and said to the mail clerk: "Are all your players locals, sir?"

"Of course," the man helping him said. "We bring in no ringers, sir, and our Blues are fine sportsmen."

After gnawing on his lip, Judge Brett commented loudly: "Playing the Bloomer Girls?"

Ruth turned to him and said: "You should come to our game, sir."

I swear, if I hadn't held Ruth in the highest regard, I would have strangled her right then and there because the man-killing judge said: "The game is to be played in . . ." He checked his watch.

The clerk volunteered the game time and told him the location: "At Stout's Pasture." The way he said it sounded like a brag as if Stout's Pasture was something like South Side Park in Chicago.

The killer of my pa slipped his watch back into his vest pocket and thanked Ruth and the postal clerk, and moved toward the door just as the old codger hollered from the back: "Here it is!"

Those words stopped the judge, who I wished would mind his own business, and, for some reason, he watched the old-timer bring the box over to me.

When he asked if I was Miss Ruth Eagan, I said: "No, I'm Lucy Totton, but Ruth is right over yonder."

I didn't turn around to point Ruth out because I knew the clerk wasn't blind and, the old woman having left, Ruth was now the only real female in the post office, and, more importantly, I didn't want Judge Brett to get a better look at my face. I started to really dislike the old fellow who hated undragged roads.

Package in hand, he said: "This must be signed for by Miss Ruth Eagan or . . ."

"Her ma," I said in defeat.

The old fellow looked up at me. "You can't be her ma." His eyes squinted and he give me a look like I'd seen folks give Russ Waddell or Buckskin or, most often fat and ugly Nelson McConnell when they were decked out in their Bloomer uniforms. Under in other circumstance, I would have been happy because I'd grown sick and tired of getting mistook for a female. He laughed and said: "Your name is *Lucy?*"

Ruth came over and said that she'd sign for her own package, because we had to leave before Mr. Norris, our manager, had a conniption.

In the meantime, the telegrapher had gone over to this box on the wall, which was a telephone I learnt, and he tried doing something to it a few times. "Thunderation, the telephone is dead, too," he said as he set down the piece he'd put against his ear, mumbling: "This is really quite mysterious."

"Had the same problem a few years back . . . during that bad winter . . . remember?" commented Mr. Sehy, the reporter.

The telegrapher said: "That was because of the snow and ice. It's summer."

The old codger stepped over by the reporter, as he said to the telegrapher: "But there's dirt and dust and wind and flies and flies and flies." Then he turned to yell at the judge to shut the fool door because there were already enough flies swarming the building. I stopped hating that bony old Methuselah when I heard the door shut, followed by footsteps on the boardwalk, which meant Judge Brett was out of my hair.

When Ruth was done signing for the parcel, Mr. Sehy asked her for another five minutes, but Ruth said she was sorry but she had to get ready for the game. She told him to come to the game, and then perhaps he could talk to other players when it was over. That's the kind of person Ruth was, considerate. Didn't matter if you was writing for the Axtell *Anchor* or *The Sporting News*, she treated you the same. Decent. Better than decent.

When Ruth and me stepped outside onto the boardwalk, I felt a mite better, and then, briefly, true happiness come over me when Ruth pulled the new-leather smelling wonderful Spalding mitt out of the box and cried: "Look . . . !" She looked even more beautiful than usual, and I almost bit my tongue because I could tell by the way her lips were forming that she was about to call me by my Christian name and not Lucy Totton. I cringed on account that Judge Brett hadn't gone no farther than a few doors down, and was standing outside Berry's Hardware. Ruth did call me by my true name, but nobody could've heard it—I barely did and I stood right beside her.

And nobody would have cared—except for the judge—because at that moment everybody in Axtell figured out why the telegraph lines was down and the telephones weren't working.

There was two banks in Axtell—the Citizens Bank and the State Bank of Axtell. The Citizens Bank had $133,667.61 in deposits and $25,000 capital, while just across the square the State Bank had "abundant capital and a fine equipment" and was "prepared to extend every reasonable accommodation." I learnt this, as did everybody else, if they happened to read the Axtell *Anchor*, 'cause these numbers and facts had been printed in that newspaper.

And that's how come the Gallagher Gang knew about the banks. Which was why, an hour or so later, Mr. Bannan, a director at the State Bank of

Axtell, and a Mr. Hostetler of the Citizens Bank, were yelling at Mr. Sehy of the *Anchor* for having printed them figures in the newspaper. Mr. Sehy told the two angry bankers that if they didn't want them numbers printed, they shouldn't have included that information in the advertisements they wanted put in the *Anchor.*

I don't know why the Bannan fellow was so mad. The Gallaghers didn't rob the State Bank, just the Citizens Bank. Guess maybe they had heard about what happened to them Daltons down in Coffeyville, and decided they best not try to rob two banks on the same day. So they had picked the Citizens Bank.

Not that it mattered all that much.

But don't believe that blood-and-thunder account written by that Colonel Bertrue some two weeks later that got published in the *Wide Awake Weekly.* I don't see how a fellow can write about a bank robbery when he wasn't even there. The reason I know he wasn't there is because he didn't mention me or Ruth or Buckskin or the Axtell Blues. He didn't write about the Kansas City Bloomer Girls, either, or even say anything about baseball in that little bitsy type. He wrote about a Marshal Fairweather, a fictional person according to Buckskin, and said there was ten Gallagher brothers, when there was only three, with only two of them being brothers. The third was a first cousin.

At least, that's how the Caney *Chronicle* had it in its story that got printed up in a Topeka newspaper when we come back down south for a ball game four days later. Colonel Bertrue got it right though when he said the Gallaghers cut the telegraph lines and broke into the telephone company where they hog-tied and gagged the two employees and messed up most of the equipment inside the office just before they rode up to the Citizens Bank.

When they come out of the bank, which is right when Ruth and me left the post office, they started shooting. I'd only been shot at once, when the rotten judge fired at me from inside my own home, but I know more bullets likely would have been sent my way had he recollected to reload the Winchester. But I can tell you the sound of these three guns being fired at the same time was a lot louder than that Winchester.

Glass was breaking. Dogs were barking. Men were screaming right along with the women. I yelled at Ruth—"Get down!"—and dived, wrapping my arms around her and pulling her behind a water trough right before a bullet fired by one of them Gallaghers smashed the plate-glass window of the post office.

Hearing that shattering glass, I rolled off of Ruth, and sneaked a glance inside where I saw the newspaper editor and the old codger diving behind the desk of the telegrapher, whose eyes were large behind his spectacles before a hand reached up, latched onto his arm, and jerked him off his stool and out of sight.

My ears were ringing from the cannonade as I looked down the boardwalk and seen Judge Brett, who wasn't looking at me, but at the Citizens Bank and the three Gallaghers, before reason come to him and he leaped into the entrance way of the hardware store.

"My new glove," Ruth whispered, but, with all the noise, my ears didn't register them words.

You see, my brain was preoccupied with that homicidal judge, wondering if it would be unchristian if I wished that a stray bullet or even an intentional one struck the man and killed him dead. Then I thought it might not matter if it was unchristian 'cause, by grab, that no-good had murdered my pa and God likely don't mind revenge in appropriate cases.

But then Ruth's words took hold of me as I felt movement behind me, and when I rolled over toward her and the water trough all I saw was the water trough. Slowly, but not too slowly because all this was happening faster than Russ Waddell's fastball when he ain't hung over, I recollected that when I had tackled Ruth, her new baseball glove flew out of her hands and over the water trough and into the street.

Cussing, I stood, and I saw Ruth bending over as deadly bullets flew all over the place. I ran around the water trough just as a bullet sent water splashing up like an oil-well gusher like the drawing I'd seen in a *Frank Leslie's Illustrated Newspaper*. Ruth scooped up her new Spalding and stood. I jumped and grabbed Ruth around the waist to pull her to safety at the same time one of them Gallaghers rode up and aimed his Colt revolver at Ruth and me.

I'm no hero. Golly, I ain't nothing but a second baseman, though I can play anywhere I'm needed but not as good as I do in the middle infield. But seeing that Colt and fearing that the bank robber was about to gun down sweet, pretty Ruth in cold blood, I shifted and flung Ruth into the water trough with her brand new Spalding first basewoman's glove.

I wanted to dive in with her, but my legs did not move.

I could see the finger of the mounted Gallagher tighten on that trigger, and I pictured myself getting shot dead, and would've been dead, too, had not a bullet just then hit him just above the second button of the bank-robbing scoundrel's calico shirt. This Gallagher—learnt later it was Charles—fell out of his saddle, along with his still cocked Colt. His body slammed right into me and drove me to the ground. I couldn't see nothing now 'cause Charles Gallagher was right on top of the upper half of my body, the tails of his duster covering my head.

Sure made them millions of flies happy as they buzzed around this carnage going on in Axtell, Kansas, on a late Wednesday afternoon in early June.

Chapter Fourteen

**DIDN'T RELISH
BLOOMER GIRLS**

—

**HORTON HEADLIGHT TELLS ALL
ABOUT THEM.**

—

BALDHEADS WERE FOOLED

—

**Some of the Girls Shave Regularly
and Chew Tobacco, in Fact
They Aren't Girls—A Sad
Look.**

—

The Leavenworth Post
Leavenworth, Kansas
June 15, 1906

Ruth Eagan was sobbing, whilst I was lying one way and the late Charles Gallagher lying the other, us forming a cross, which seemed foreboding to her because it implied that we had gone to Glory together.

While I couldn't see anything, I could still hear the shouting and the guns firing all around me.

"What's the number of the police department?"

"Fifty-eight!"

157

"That's the doc's telephone number!"

"Might as well call him, too!"

Horses screamed. The one that had been rode by the late Charles Gallagher was stomping and had I been thinking right I would have done all I could do to get out from beneath that dead outlaw, and move behind that trough or inside it with Ruth and her new baseball glove. See, I wasn't thinking much about nothing but visualizing what I'd seen out of the corner of my eye moments before that blood sprayed like a geyser from the dying Charles Gallagher's chest.

What I'd seen was a girl, a big girl, standing beside a wagon at the train depot, working the lever of a rifle, and bringing that rifle up slowly, and aiming at the man who was pointing a Colt at me and Ruth.

"Buckskin," I mouthed.

Buckskin Compton had shot that outlaw dead, and that's when I recalled that conversation I wasn't sure I'd actually heard on the train to Axtell. Now I understood that I hadn't dreamt that, no sir. That was what I was thinking till somebody shifted Gallagher off me, sending flies buzzing. It was another Gallagher. And he was kneeling by Charles, and crying out: "Charlie. Oh, Charlie!"

Then a bullet slapped the hitching rail just behind him and me, and a second dug up dirt that I could feel hit the soles of my shoes. The

Gallagher who was crying aimed his pistol at the shooter and shot twice.

That's when somebody yelled—"Don't move,"—punctuating that order with a few prime cuss words.

Then I heard water splashing and Ruth coughing, spitting out water, and softly saying my name. This Gallagher heard her, too, and he knew Axtell's lawmen as well as a number of citizens who'd taken liberty of rifles and shotguns and revolvers inside that hardware store were closing in on him.

"You're all that's left. The other two are dead," said one of the lawmen. "You'd best give yourself . . ."

"Not Thomas, too," he muttered. Maybe it was the fear of prison, but whatever it was, this Gallagher, the cousin Jenks, made a dash to the water trough.

"Get away from me or the wench dies!" he ordered, his gun in his hand.

I started to sit up, planning to dive and tackle him and beat him so that there wouldn't be nothing left even to satisfy the millions of flies buzzing around Axtell, but I didn't get a chance because a whistling sounded, then a smacking noise, and then a groan from Jenks Gallagher as he dropped his revolver into the trough, and the last of them Gallaghers fell onto the boardwalk in front of the post office.

The ball that Katie Maloney had thrown, which had smacked Jenks in his temple and could have killed him deader than his two cousins, rolled next to Charles Gallagher's gun hand.

The citizens of Axtell who had gathered up and down the street went crazy.

Which was a good thing, because as I finally sat up, a drenched Ruth sloshed out of the trough, not even bothering to fetch her new glove, and sank onto her knees beside me. She pulled my head against her bosom, sobbing and thanking the Almighty that I'd been delivered. She used my given name a couple of times, which made me worry someone would hear her, but then she stopped and just stared at me with them lovely eyes of hers. She must've figured out that the folks gathering around still thought that all of us Bloomer Girls was truly females, so she stroked my hair and said: "Poor, poor, Lucy."

She no more than got out those three words when her ma come along and snatched the baseball mitt out of the trough and pointed a long finger at me, saying: "How could you?" And she informed me that the glove was a Number BXS—which ain't numbers unless they's some of them Roman numerals that I don't quite grasp—and that it cost four whole dollars. She paused and then started to say something else but Ruth shut her up with one word.

"Mother."

Right then is when Buckskin, carrying not a big Winchester but his bat bag, come up to me, squatted, and asked: "You hit?"

I shook my head feebly.

Then somebody asked Gypsie O'Hearn: "I saw one of them female players shooting. Was it you?"

Gypsie replied: "You're drunk!"

Policemen, the doctor whose phone number was fifty-eight, a photographer whose name was Condiff, and the tellers and officers of both banks had flocked to the street by now. Those who had never heard of the Gallaghers got all worked up when they realized their town had been attacked by a gang.

The mayor appeared and he said the ball game would have to be canceled. This sure put Mr. Norris into a bad mood, but most of us understood there wasn't no way we'd be selling many tickets or programs on a day like today. Not when the citizens were interested only in the Gallaghers and what had taken place that afternoon. Those who had witnessed it didn't have to be coaxed very hard to tell the story over and over again.

"This'll show Coffeyville," one of the city boosters said, but it didn't show Coffeyville nothing because nobody outside of Marshall County had ever heard of the notorious Gallaghers. Besides, there was only three of them, and only two of them dead, and nobody else in town had gotten hurt. Mr. Sehy said he'd be danged if he'd put this kind of news in his paper because the *Anchor*'s motto was **Advertising is to Business What Steam is to Machinery—The Grand Motive Power**. He believed that nobody would advertise or move to a town where lawlessness ran rampant, and he didn't want Axtell, Kansas, in 1906, to be regarded as Dodge City, Caldwell, Bloody Newton, or one of them other scandalous cattle towns back in the previous century.

With the game canceled, Mr. Norris told the crew to hurry and take down our canvas fences and grandstand over in Stout's Pasture and see if they could get them on the next eastbound.

"Eastbound?" I said, and didn't use my girl's voice, even though I was still standing near the post office.

"Yes," with a few cusses before and after was the answer of Mr. Norris. So that meant Maryville, Hiawatha, and St. Joseph, but at least none of them towns was Pleasanton.

I asked: "Ain't we ever going west?"

He said: "Sure. After Caney."

But Caney, where I'd played as a ringer two or three times, wasn't west at all, but south, down around the border, seventy miles from Pleasanton, not far by train. I started to ask something else, but shut my big mouth, fearing the judge might have recognized me and could be hanging around and trying to find out where we'd be playing— and where he, with or without the evil Widow Amy DeFee, could end my season permanent.

Then a bigger thing came along to bother me. The chief of the Axtell police said he would need statements from everybody, and our addresses, in case we had to come back to testify in the trial of Jenks Gallagher.

So someone asked: "Does anyone know where Judge Stovall is?"

Someone sniggered, saying: "I expect Miss Candy's . . . this being Wednesday."

Which left everybody uncomfortable except for Nelse McConnell who figured out what that meant right quick. He asked the sniggering gent: "Where's Miss Candy's?"

"Where the North Fork of the Black Vermillion meets Clear Creek," said the old codger from the post office, which makes plenty of sense because a fellow who had to deliver the mail would know where most folks live.

"Let's go have a look around," McConnell said, but Waddell said it was too close to leaving time.

At this, the lawman said nobody was going nowhere till he got statements from the witnesses.

Mr. Ed Norris insisted that the Bloomer Girls go first on account they had to catch the 532, which was leaving at 5:05 p.m.

At this, Maggie Casey glared at Mr. Norris and

asked: "How were we supposed to play a game at three o'clock and catch that train?"

"If you want to run this team, make me an offer!" Mr. Ed Norris fired back.

Buckskin had to step in front of Mr. Norris whilst Pearl Murphy, Maude Sullivan, Carrie Cassady, and Agnes McGuire held back Maggie Casey, who looked like she wanted to rip off Mr. Norris's head and then spit into the hole.

When the chief said we were wasting time, a voice said: "I'm a judge, if you need help."

The lawman seemed obliged whilst I felt like getting my Hawthorne and just riding as far away from Axtell as I could.

My stomach begun knotting up as that low-down, pa-killing Kevin Brett stepped over to the police chief and shook his hand, introducing hisself. He told the lawman he was willing to oversee or assist in the taking of statements.

Ruth was the first to tell what she had witnessed after we came out of the post office. Luckily she hadn't seen Buckskin shoot Charles Gallagher dead. For all I knew, Buckskin might have also shot Gallagher's brother Thomas.

When it was my turn, I got touchy, having to put my hand on a Bible and swearing to tell the truth, the whole truth, and nothing but the truth, and then lying with the first words out of my mouth after I got asked: "What's your name?"

"Lucy Totton." I'd never tried to sound more like a girl than I done right then.

"Age?"

"Twenty-one."

I was batting a thousand in the lying department.

"Residence?"

"The Kansas City Bloomer Girls." That's what Ruth and four other Bloomer Girls had answered before I had to talk.

"Tell what you saw," Brett said, looking up as he wrote down my information. I wet my lips and then started to talk, trying to keep it brief. Here I was, not wearing no disguise, not even a wig, sitting before the murderer of my pa, a mad-dog killer who had known me for years, though he had never seen me decked out like some female. The judge cocked his head, and I figured I was dead, but Gypsie O'Hearn—bless her—picked that moment to roll up her bloomer leg and scratch her calf. She might not have been the most attractive female on our team, but her limbs were right healthy—you'll remember she trapped me with her limbs on the train. What I'm trying to say is that Kevin Brett didn't pay that much attention to me or what I was saying, especially once I explained that Charles Gallagher fell on top of me.

Quicker than some of my at-bats when I was slumping, my testimony was finished. The telegrapher who'd volunteered to help had me sign and date my statement. The judge seemed to be studying me, so I tried to remain calm and respectful as I gave that cold-blooded killer a nod and grabbed my bag and walked out of the furniture store, where we had gathered when the owner volunteered his building so folks could sit while waiting to give their statements.

Maybe things would've gone all right, if Nelse McConnell, Russ Waddell, and even my pard, Buckskin Compton, hadn't given their statements to the judge, too. Because, according to Waddell, once McConnell had turned in his statement, the telegrapher had said: "If that's a girl, I'm Carrie Nation."

"What makes you say that?" the judge had asked.

"There's tobacco flecks in her teeth."

Judge Brett said: "My grandmother dipped snuff, sir."

"But I bet she wasn't badly in need of a shave," the telegrapher said.

I feared that would get the judge a-thinking.

We traveled to Caney without incident. But during the game the next day I kept looking into the stands, fearing I'd see either Judge Brett or the Widow Amy DeFee. Or not see nothing, and just get kilt. Well, I didn't hit worth a fip. I mishandled routine ground balls. Overthrew to Ruth and made her jump to try to catch the baseball with her new Spalding glove, which the soaking in the trough didn't do much harm to.

When we got to the hotel, Waddell and McConnell went off to try to find a place like Miss Candy's over where the North Fork of the Black Vermillion meets Clear Creek. Buckskin stayed behind with me.

He pulled a chair over beside my bed, where I was curled up, trying not to shake or cry.

"Let's talk," he said.

Chapter Fifteen

The Caney Glass Company shut down its plant yesterday after the best and most successful fire of any plant in the business, and the shutting down was a couple of days ahead of schedule time, on account of the Bloomer ball game.

When Manager Thornburg went out to the four o'clock shift, not a soul was there. He searched the entire plant over, and finally found one lonely fellow on duty, and he could not blow a cylinder. It was Clerk Bruce Hinkle. No one showed up, and Fred went out and turned out the fires and declared the thing off.

The boys could not withstand the temptation to see the Bloomer girls play ball, and all were at the game.

Caney Chronicle
Caney, Kansas
June 8, 1906

I'd heard all of Buckskin's talks, so when Buckskin said: "Maybe you would have rather had me let that hard-rock bank robber shoot you and Miss Ruth back in Axtell."

I stopped my sniffling and lifted my head off the pillow, which wasn't comfortable nohow but somewhat softer than what they stuffed the mattresses with in this rawhide hotel—it sure wasn't straw.

"Sit up," Buckskin told me.

I sat up, swung my legs off the bed.

"Look at me."

Done that, too.

"Well?" he said.

"Ain't sorry that me and Ruth . . . sorry, Ruth and me . . . ain't dead. So, thanks."

He gave a slight nod. "You've been nervous since you joined this team. So have Miss Ruth, Miss Carrie, and even the ladies with a lot of experience. To tell the truth, turkey vultures still flap their wings in my belly before every game. When you aren't nervous, it's time to hang up you glove and spikes."

I looked at my fingernails, the way a fellow is prone to study them, but not to mock Buckskin, just to do something other than look Buckskin in the eye. He didn't say nothing about it, didn't scold me and remind me that that ain't how ladies look at their nails. Instead, he asked straight-out: "Are you a runaway?"

My hand lowered. "My parents are dead."

"That's not what I asked."

Well, looking at him again, I almost started to tell him, but my lips got to trembling and that lump come up into my throat. I turned my head toward the far corner of the room where a big spider sat in its web. I studied it a moment, and then turned my head to watch the curtains fluttering in the open window—it was hot, and the breeze wasn't doing no good cooling down the room. My neck had a crick from that pillow, so I rubbed it before turning to look at Buckskin again.

He said: "Maybe I should be honest with you."

Which he was—unless he was lying, which wasn't in Buckskin's nature.

"My name," he said, "is Ulysses Howard Skinner." He pronounced it YULI-sees, not YOU-liss-es, but he explained that, too. "My dad wore the blue, served under Grant, but he married a girl from Arkansas and moved to Fort Smith long after the war. I was born in 'Eighty. He insisted on naming me after his commanding general, but you can't be called YOU-liss-es in Arkansas without getting your arse pummeled, so I was YULI-sees, till I got sick of that. Then I became Howard . . . till I got nicknamed Buck. And I don't remember how that came about, but it stuck."

"Buck Skinner," I said. "Buckskin." I caught on real quick.

"Yeah. Mother's maiden name was Compton."

"Where did Bill come from?"

"Plucked it from the sky."

That got me to pondering how come I'd never done that kind of considering before. Why should I keep the name Pa and Ma give me? Why couldn't I just call myself something new? All sorts of names come to my mind, but they were names other folks had already took for themselves: Wild Bill . . . Buffalo Bill . . . Pawnee Bill . . . Bad Bill . . . Wee Willie . . . Old Reliable, though I wasn't old, or reliable . . . Deacon, who I didn't like on account he played for the New York Highlanders in the American League, but, dang, if he didn't have the most awesomest curveball in baseball unless all those newspapers and even *The Sporting News* was exaggerating or just plain lying. Then I thought maybe just Kid, seeing that's what most of the Bloomer Girls called me anyway, when they weren't calling me Lucy that is.

I asked Buckskin: "But ain't Buckskin too close to Buck Skinner?"

He shrugged. "I use it, 'cause it's an easy handle for me to remember. If I called myself Oglethorpe Aloysius"—he grinned—"I'd likely forget, and that can get a man on the dodge in trouble. Buckskin . . . well I'm used to it. If someone called out Buck Skinner, I'd just keep on walking. I've taught myself to do that. Bill's easy enough to remember. Compton was, as I said, my mother's name before she married. And if things get hot, I can always find another name. Bill Compton isn't the first name I've taken as my own."

"What do you mean by hot?" I asked, even though I'd already guessed how Buckskin would answer that one, if he was really being truthful.

"Because there are men who'd like to see Buck Skinner dead."

Just like there was a murdering jurist and a no-good, evil and just plain wicked, black-hearted widow who wanted me dead. Buckskin and me had a bond.

The way Buckskin told the story was that he had left Fort Smith when he was around my age, made it to Pueblo, Colorado, where he played part-time for the Rovers.

When he come up to Leadville—which was hurting all them years after the Panic of '93, whatever that was—he found something he was good at.

"I'd hunted supper with a shotgun back in Arkansas, but Pa never owned a rifle," he said. "There was a shooting contest over the Fourth of July and an old-timer I kinda knew loaned me his rifle. I won."

That got him a job hunting game for hotel restaurants for a while. He found a better job doing the same thing back in Pueblo, but, this

172

being 1899, there wasn't no Colorado State League no more, so he didn't play much baseball. He hunted, became a better marksman, and got deputized by marshals after two bad men escaped from the pen in Cañon City, west of Pueblo. That's where he shot one of the escapees in the leg on the Arkansas River, which Buckskin pronounced ARE-kan-sas because he hailed from Arkansas. Everybody else knows it's actually pronounced Are-KAN-sas unless you come from Arkansas.

"Well, that ain't a bad thing, is it?" I asked, not meaning how he pronounced Arkansas but rather shooting a fellow who escaped from prison.

"Considering what the man was in the pen for, I didn't think so," Buckskin said. "And the marshals were pleased."

They patched up the convict's leg, and trapped his partner on a sandbar who give hisself up without no need for no more shooting.

The next year, though, Buckskin got hired up in Sweetwater County in Wyoming, which is where he met Tom Horn, who I never met nor heard of and never will get to meet on account that in 1903 they hanged him—not hung him, as Buckskin told me, explaining that a man is *hanged* but a picture is *hung*.

Well, I knew they hanged him because I'd overheard Mr. Norris say they had hanged Horn using a Julian Gallows back on the train.

They hanged Tom Horn, Buckskin said, because he shot a fourteen-year-old boy, Willie Nickel, who he might've mistook for the kid's pa. Then some lawman got Horn drunk to get him talking. Horn talked, and what he said didn't help him at his trial. The lawman who got him drunk said that Horn told him that the shot that killed the boy was done at a range of three hundred yards, and that: "It was the best shot I ever made, and the dirtiest trick I ever done."

The jury found Horn guilty. The judge sentenced him to die and he did die after they *hanged* him three years back.

I was feeling sort of sick to my stomach, even though I knew nothing about this kid who got kilt by mistake. I asked: "Did Tom Horn really kill that boy?"

I asked him that even though I feared he was going to tell me, no, Tom was innocent for it was I, Ulysses Howard Skinner, who murdered the boy just as I'm going to murder you. I guess the reason that ugly idea come to mind was that I recollected that train-ride conversation where Mr. Norris said Buckskin had shot two riders dead at four hundred yards.

But Buckskin didn't say that, and, besides, he said the kid was kilt with a .30-30, and I knew Buckskin used a .45-90. The Widow Amy DeFee owned a .30-30, but I don't think she kilt Willie Nickel even though I wouldn't put it past her.

"I don't know," Buckskin said. "I wasn't there."

You see, he had up and quit that big ranch up in Wyoming that had hired him as a stock detective—which meant shooting nesters in cold blood which went against Buckskin's nature—so he wasn't even around when Tom Horn, or somebody, murdered Willie Nickel, a boy two years younger than I was.

Anyway, Buckskin found hisself in the Powder River country, where nobody knew nothing about baseball. That surprised me because you'd think that a state that thought enough to let women vote and hold office would be smart enough to play baseball. Buckskin explained that it was too windy to play baseball in Wyoming, 'cause that wind would create havoc with the ball.

Living all my life in Kansas, I figured I knew all there was to know about wind, but I'm sure glad not to hail from Wyoming.

That Powder River country job got Buckskin in trouble. He met a woman—didn't tell me her name—who had three brothers. Those fellows didn't cotton to Buckskin and his buggy rides with their sister, so they beat him up right bad and left him to die. 'Course, Buckskin didn't die and he went back to the ranch and whupped one of the brothers bad, then rode away from the woman he loved because he didn't want the two brothers to take out their meanness on her. But them two brothers who didn't get whupped went

175

after Buckskin, and when they found him, they started shooting. Buckskin shot them dead out at four hundred yards, which I had already heard on the train to Axtell from Mr. Norris.

"But ain't that self-defense?" I asked.

Buckskin smiled. "Their father is a judge, so I didn't take any chances."

Another bond. The Widow Amy DeFee's pard was a judge, too.

"Didn't you want to take the girl with you?" I asked him.

"After breaking one brother's nose, jaw, and the fingers on his right hand? Then shooting her other two brothers dead? Those kind of things put a damper on a woman's feelings, kid."

After that, Buckskin drifted, hid out, and then in August of 1903 he happened to be in Colorado Springs, Colorado, when the Keystones were playing the Bloomer Girls. That's when he met up with Mr. Norris and come up with the name Bill "Buckskin" Compton, alias Dolly Madison. He'd been hiding out with a mostly girl baseball team ever since.

"What about that marshal, you knew?" I asked when Buckskin stopped talking. "The Dalton brother . . . the lawman who was kin to them fellows that got shot down like dogs over in Coffeyville."

I remembered that because Caney, where we was, weren't no more than twenty miles west of

Coffeyville, which reminded me that Caney was maybe a hundred and forty miles southwest of Pleasanton, and if Judge Brett could find his way to Axtell, which was maybe two hundred miles northwest of Pleasanton, then surely he could find Caney, especially if he'd overheard where we was going to be playing next.

"Frank Dalton?" Buckskin smiled. "I met Frank when I was a kid. Just once. I'm what . . . six, seven . . . we were playing baseball in the streets. No bats. We used our hands."

That left me thunderstruck. No bats. Russ Waddell had told me that he used a tobacco stick when he was a kid, and I told that to Buckskin who said that Russ come from South Carolina, where they grow tobacco, and farming was a lot more profitable than what Buck's dad done for a living. He didn't say what kind of work his pa done, although I knew he had tried to do something with turkeys, but I reckon it didn't make him rich.

"No baseball, either," Buckskin continued. "We were too poor to own a baseball. We wadded up torn pages from a newspaper."

Now, that sounded dirt poor, and it got me to thinking that the Widow Amy DeFee and my pa had bought me gloves and bats and balls and even a Hawthorne bicycle to get me to games all across southern Kansas. Though the first time I played in Caney, I'd come down by train with the Widow Amy DeFee because she said she had some business over in Tyro.

"Frank Dalton scared the tar out of us," Buckskin said, and he did say tar. "Well, I guess it was that badge that he wore that scared us. I had just rifled a ball into the street off of David Ward. Dalton picked it up and said . . . 'Keep it up, son. Baseball will take you places.'

"Marshal Dalton walked to his horse. A clerk outside one of the stores said . . . 'You boys best listen to Marshal Dalton and watch that you don't get hurt playing in these streets.' "

That's how Buckskin learnt the marshal's name and how come he felt sad two weeks later when the whole town mourned Deputy Marshal Frank Dalton's murder.

That was Buckskin's story.

After checking his watch, he said: "Your turn, kid."

CHAPTER SIXTEEN

Considerable opposition has arisen in some quarters to the game of base ball advertised to occur at the fair grounds on Sunday, June 10, between the local team and a so-called "Bloomer Girl" bunch, and the aid of the county peace officers has been invoked to prevent it. County Attorney Sturges can find no law against Sunday base ball games and has so informed the complainants, but not satisfied with his opinion a request has been made, through him, for a ruling on the question by Attorney General Coleman.

The Daily Blade
Concordia, Kansas
June 1, 1906

I didn't take near as long as Buckskin had to tell my story 'cause it didn't cover years, just weeks. There ain't no need to recite all I told Buckskin, 'cause if you've come this far in my narrative, you already know how I became

Lucy Totton and joined the Bloomer Girls.

We were both on the run from evil folks, and after I'd told him pretty much everything, he nodded solemnly, leaned forward, shook his head.

"Kid, why on earth didn't you tell the Axtell police chief? He could've arrested that judge and gotten a warrant issued for your stepmother."

My head moved back and forth, hard and fast like it does when any umpire calls a ball four inches off the plate a strike. I know I can't let an umpire know my thoughts about his call, so I just shake my head. To the umpire it may look like that means I'm thinking—*By thunder, I can't believe I let that pitch go*—but what it really means, but could never get proved, is that I was disputing the accuracy of the umpire's judgment.

"No, no, no, no," I kept saying whilst my head shook, giving Buckskin the pitifullest look I could muster. "Nobody's gonna believe me. I'm sixteen years old, and you ain't never met the Widow Amy DeFee. She ain't like Ruth. She ain't like that gal you took a shine to in the Powder River Country. By thunder, she's meaner than Maggie Casey. Grown men think she's kind and loving, when she's the vilest, repulsivest, meanest, contemptiblist . . ."

Buckskin held out his hand, so I stopped talking for maybe two seconds before I started up again.

"You ain't never met her, Buck. You don't know what all she can do. And maybe you ought to think about what would happen if the law found out about me and her. The newspapers, too . . . they'd start reporting that all of us Bloomer Girls ain't really females."

Buckskin grinned. "They've been doing that . . . most of them . . . since I joined the team almost three years ago."

"But they'd be writing about you, too. They'd be asking you questions about me. They'd be wanting to print whatever name you come up with."

His smile disappeared. "I see your point," Buckskin said, though I ain't sure he did because he also said: "Are you absolutely certain this is how you want to play this hand?"

Not being certain about nothing, I just nodded on account that McConnell and Waddell entered the room and said that Caney, Kansas, had to be the worst town they'd ever struck. They said that you couldn't find nothing but factories that made bricks and glass, plus smelters that smelted lead and zinc, and oil wells and wells that brung up natural gas, and that the whole county stunk worser than Sour Lake, Texas. They suggested that Kansas would be wise if they'd just cede this whole parcel of ground to the Osage Indians for it wasn't good for nothing excepting holding the ends of the earth together.

But I'll tell you something pure gospel. Caney might have stunk of oil and gas and bricks and glass and lead and zinc and goober peas, which are plumb disgusting, but the folks sure piled out to watch us Bloomer Girls play baseball against the home boys. The gate receipts made Mr. Norris and I quote, "happier than a pig in clover." Being from a railroad town, I don't know much about pigs nor clover.

Whilst my little talk with Buckskin maybe inspired me to play ball slightly better that day, all in all, we done pretty good, and Mr. Norris was real happy.

That didn't last once we reached Concordia, where Mr. Norris learnt that the city, county, and state objected to playing baseball games on a Sunday, so Concordia refused to play us. Our quick thinking and angry manager scheduled a game in St. Paul, instead.

If you ain't from Kansas, eastern Kansas especially, then you might not know that St. Paul, Kansas, is maybe eighty miles from Pleasanton, which ain't as close to the Widow Amy DeFee as Fort Scott, where I joined the Bloomer Girls, but, by road, it is closer than Chanute. It was nearer than I wanted to be.

My worries came true because the widow showed up at the ball game. Brung the judge with her. Took some doing, because the game weren't played in St. Paul, but at R.S. McGowen's pasture. The fact that St. Paul had a railroad line going to it, but R.S. McGowen's farm didn't, might be the only reason I'm alive to write this.

We were playing the Valley Boys, and all the folks in St. Paul said they were the fastest ballists in the whole state, which might be true. But the folks in St. Paul don't just put on a baseball game. Before I throwed the first pitch—I was taking over for Waddell who was feeling plumb miserable and said he'd have to get better just to die—they showed off their starting nine and their muffin nine by having them run foot races. They put on what they called fat man's races in which their catcher and two muffins beat some old men and two younger ones who must've each weighed three hundred pounds. None of them ballists ran in the Ladies Egg Race as none of them was women, of course, but they did take part in the tug-of-war contest, they rolled ten pins in an alley somebody had erected just for the baseball game, and finally they went to the shooting gallery. They topped it off by having refreshments, which included not only velvet ice cream from Brogan's parlor but also ice cream freezers from C.M. Koenig's place.

Four of their players got so sick, the umpire called the game after seven innings, which is what saved my life, because the Widow Amy DeFee, her man-killing judge, plus a couple of fellows who must've been hired by her, had trouble finding out where the game was being held.

They got there after the Valley Boys—the sick, the feeble, and the just plain tuckered-out players—were leaving. The grandstand and canvas fences were already down and being put into wagons. And us Bloomer Girls was preparing to ride over to the depot and take the westbound Katy.

Standing behind the wagon that held our grips, I heard the Widow Amy DeFee's voice: "Excuse me, kind sir, but I am seeking my runaway son." Made me almost as sick as them Valley Boys was.

I held my breath as she continued to talk, figuring Brett must have recognized me back in Axtell, after all. Heard her say: "We have reason to believe that he is pretending to be a Bloomer Girl."

Still wearing my uniform, I figured I was dead, certain sure.

Yet luck was with me, because my grip with both my female clothing and my man duds was just inside the wagon, so I jumped into the back of it. I thanked the Almighty that the canvas tarp would allow me to get out of my Bloomer outfit and put on my suit bought back in Emporia. I left my bat and my glove and everything that would have identified me as a Bloomer Girl and hightailed it out of the wagon, trying not to act like I wasn't about to die of no apoplexy.

"Hey, you!" the Widow Amy DeFee called out.

I kept walking, but glanced back and saw she was looking at Pearl Murphy, who was about my height, had my hair color even if hers was longer and curlier than mine. Pearl stopped, though I don't know why she did. As she stood there, one of the widow's gunmen strode up to her and ripped off her ball cap and pulled her hair. This made Pearl yell, made me grimace and feel ashamed to see that fine outfielder getting abused on account of me.

I would've stopped and come to Pearl's rescue, but Nelse McConnell, four Valley Boys who weren't that sick, the pasture owner, and two Osage Indians who'd come up to watch baseball and eat ice cream freezers, two deputies, and four of our crew all ran to protect Pearl Murphy. When the cur who'd manhandled our left fielder reached for the revolver he wore high on his hip, the Widow Amy DeFee hollered: "Walt Coburn, don't be a fool!" That stopped him, as did a deputy who had drawn his revolver and aimed it at Walt Coburn. Meanwhile, the other deputy had his gun pointed at the other fellow the widow had brought.

The Widow Amy DeFee tried to explain, but by then Maggie Casey had come up and kicked the fellow who had been rude, disrespectful, and plumb vicious to Pearl Murphy right between his legs. It took the farmer, an Osage, and one of the Valley Boys to pull Maggie off that gunman.

Though I had slowed and was glancing back every few seconds, I kept on walking, sweating till I was wetter than a bluegill. Kept walking all those miles to the depot, and got on the train, and knew I'd escaped certain death. The widow and her hired men were detained by the lawmen long enough that the Katy moved out, taking us to our next town.

When I told Buckskin, who hadn't seen the ruction, what had happened, he told me I'd done the right thing by not trying to assist Pearl Murphy, because had the Widow Amy DeFee recognized me for certain, there likely would've been shooting, and innocent folks could've been hurt, or even killed. Including me.

Buckskin also said: "Kid, we must get you out of Kansas."

Did I mention that we won that game fair and square?

CHAPTER SEVENTEEN

Charlie Barngrover, the once-upon-a-time Dodge City baseball pitcher, has joined the "National bloomers" and is wearing bloomers and appearing as "Lady Rupert, one of the two World Reknowned lady pitchers".

The Globe-Republican
Dodge City, Kansas
July 26, 1906

E d," Buckskin asked Mr. Norris, "what have you done about scheduling games in Colorado?"

Reading over some newspapers he'd found on the seat aboard the train, Mr. Norris looked up as Buckskin and me slid into the seats across from him.

"Why?"

"Maybe I'm homesick."

Mr. Norris give Buckskin the longest stare, glanced at me no longer than an eye-blink takes, before saying: "Isn't Colorado a little close to Wyoming for you, Buck?"

"I'll take my chances."

Our manager shook his head. "I won't. I can

make my pile milking rubes for twenty-five cents a head, plus programs, plus concessions, plus appearance fees, and wagers. Sweat, hayseeds, Carrie Nation, and bank robbers aside, I sorta like Kansas."

Meaning, once we reached Lawrence, I'd have to take my Hawthorne and pedal west, hard. But, golly, how'd I miss Ruth. And Buckskin. And all my teammates, even Maggie Casey, especially since she had sent Walt Coburn, one of the Widow Amy DeFee's gunmen, to the sawbones in St. Paul with a ruptured something that sounded awful painful.

"Nickel and dime stuff," Buckskin said. "Towns of four hundred, six hundred. Denver tops a hundred thousand these days. More than twenty thousand in Colorado Springs. Pueblo's pushing thirty thousand."

"That's more than our grandstand can hold." Thinking he was funny, though also accurate, Mr. Norris chuckled.

"More people, more bets, more money for you," Buckskin said.

"Maybe, but I've got games scheduled across Kansas for the rest of this month." Mr. Norris yanked a wad of yellow telegraph papers from a coat pocket. "And offers from . . ." He glanced at one, grinned, handing it over to Buckskin. "Just look at this one. Whiting wants to play us in a doubleheader. We play the muffins from Whiting, then we play Kickapoo Indians. I'm thinking we can kick some Kickapoo hinies." No, he didn't say *hinies*.

"You'd swindle your own mother."

"Before she swindled me," Mr. Norris said, shoving the invitations and offers back inside his pocket before fetching a handkerchief from his vest pocket which he used to mop his face.

"It's cooler in the mountains," Buckskin tried another approach.

"What are you getting at?"

"Send me to Colorado. I know some baseball folks, know the towns. I'll get at least two weeks of games in the state for July."

Shaking his head, Mr. Norris dropped his soggy handkerchief and pulled out a ratty-looking notepad, which he opened. He thumbed through some pages, reading out loud the games he had already scheduled for July 3rd in Wichita, and another game which they were already calling "Women's Rights In Operation," which made me blurt out: "The girls will like that."

It was true, but Buckskin gave me a mean look, and I flattened my lips as long as I could, before I yawned 'cause this train kept *clickety-clacking*, and I was plumb tuckered out.

Mr. Norris said that he had games scheduled through July 14th, where, in Dodge City, we'd be playing Carol Lord's Swatters with Colonel Floyd Manary umpiring. That name meant nothing to me or Buckskin. Don't know if our manager had ever heard of him, either, but somebody in Dodge City must have thought the colonel to be real important, else they wouldn't have mentioned him in no telegraph.

"Perfect," Buckskin said. "I'll have us games across Colorado after the Fourteenth."

"And who plays third base while you're out traipsing across the Rocky Mountains?" Mr. Norris directed a long stare at me, before saying: "Lucy Totton here?"

"The kid'll be with me," Buckskin said.

Mr. Norris's head bobbed. "Yeah, that's what I figured. This volunteering to help me do my job wouldn't happen to have anything to do with that commotion back in Saint Paul, would it?"

Buckskin give our manager a dumb look.

Which caused Mr. Norris to glare at Buckskin as he said: "From what I heard, there was some mention of a woman trying to find a runaway."

Now Buckskin's eyes turned cold, and I mean a hard, long, freezing look, like the bluest norther that ever blew through Kansas.

Mr. Norris looked away for a moment, sighed, and tried to sound like he gave a whit about anything other than a profit. "We're going to lose Waddell, Buck. I warned him about who he . . ." Giving me a quick glance, he swallowed down what he was about to say, but it wasn't nothing I hadn't heard before since I'd been rooming with

Waddell and McConnell. I recollected Waddell complaining about what he thought some hussy—Waddell's word—had give him in Chanute, and that's why he had to go see that doctor in Dodge City, and how come by the time the Bloomer Girls joined Buckskin and me in Las Animas, Colorado, in July, Russ "Lady" Waddell had been replaced by Charlie Barngrover and Lady Rupert, who were one in the same, of course.

There I go again, as Buckskin says, getting ahead of myself.

Buckskin reminded Mr. Norris: "You found me in Colorado Springs. Picked up Nelse in Omaha, signed Russ down in the Indian Nations, and the kid in . . ."

"Mound City," I said, but then scrunched up my eyes, trying to remember. "Or maybe Fort Scott, technically, since that's where I first suited up."

Buckskin told Mr. Norris: "You can find a player anywhere."

"But I'd be out two men till I found a couple of desperate men short on cash and pride."

"You have enough for a battery. That's all it really takes. Pitcher and catcher."

"If I don't find a replacement for Waddell in time . . ."

Buckskin waved his hand. "You'll be saving money. That's something I know you like. And the girls will be getting more playing time, more experience."

That's when Mr. Norris grinned, showing his yellowed teeth, and, smirking, he leaned forward and whispered to Buckskin though not soft enough that I couldn't hear.

"That woman in St. Paul . . . what if she comes to another game? Wichita . . . Newton . . . Whitney . . ."

Buckskin shrugged. "She won't find a runaway, will she?"

"Uhn-huh. I didn't see her in Saint Paul. What would I tell her if she asked me about a runaway Kansas kid?"

My belly got all sickly inside, and I felt chilled though it remained hotter than blazes.

"What could you tell her?" Buckskin said. "You don't know anything about a runaway. But here's something you do know."

Mr. Norris waited. So did I. Buckskin told him in a voice even softer than one of Carrie Cassady's whispers. Yet I heard it. And it made me shiver, though Buckskin made that threat to protect me.

"You know about Wilbur and Thad Shoumacher being shot dead off their horses at four hundred yards with an Eighteen-Eighty-Six Winchester, which has the trajectory of one of your pop-ups."

Next thing I knew, Mr. Norris was leaning way back in his seat, his face pasty-looking. He started sweating as Buckskin stared, not even blinking. I wondered if Buckskin really meant what he'd just told Mr. Norris, even though he said nothing, just reminded him about something that had happened some years back.

A good long while passed, followed by too many bobs of Mr. Norris's Adam's apple to count, before he pulled out that soaked-through handkerchief and wiped his face again.

He looked at Buckskin, but not at me, and said: "I'll have some expense money for you when we reach the station. And the schedule. Let me know by telegraph when you've got us games. Remember though, we need to be in Wallace by the second week in August as we make our way back to Kansas City to finish the season. Deal?"

Buckskin nodded. He stood. So did I. We started to walk away, but Mr. Norris said: "And one more thing. No oysters in Las Animas. Last time we were there, I was sicker than a dog for five days."

"Anybody who eats oysters in Las Animas, Colorado, deserves to get sick," Buckskin told him. And we walked to our Pullman to get some shut-eye, though I couldn't sleep that night, even aboard a train.

When we stepped off the train, Buckskin set down his grip and filled his lungs with air, let it out, and smiled. "Smell that," he said. "Do you know what that smells like?"

"Cow dung," I told him, though I didn't really

193

say *dung* because I'd been playing professional baseball with the Bloomer Girls and salty talkers like Nelse McConnell, Russ Waddell, and Maggie Casey for about a month.

Buckskin laughed. "That, kid, is the smell of the West."

Smelt like cow dung to me.

We were in Wichita, which Buckskin said once had a reputation that anything goes and was wild, woolly, and filled with cowboys, gamblers, and vice. Now it was filled with odors of cattle waiting to be slaughtered and shipped off to feed folks.

"Did you ever cowboy?" I asked.

His head shook. "Just shot cowboys."

He poked the brim of my Bloomer Girls ballcap to show that he was joshing, but I ain't altogether certain he wasn't serious. Anyway, we weren't in Wichita longer than it took us to catch another train, and soon we was in Dodge City, which had been a rip-snorting cattle town. When we got there in June of 1906 it didn't stink like Wichita, most likely 'cause it didn't have no meat-packing facility at the stockyards, so it smelt like alfalfa.

We checked out the baseball game, and, after that travesty—Buckskin's word—I could understand why Carol Lord's Swatters was so jo-fired to have Colonel Floyd Manary do the umpiring. He was either blind or a cheater, and whilst I ain't saying he was ignorant of the rules, I am saying he was both. I was relieved I wouldn't be in Dodge City when he umpired that game the Swatters had scheduled against the Bloomer Girls, though I already felt sorry for sweet Ruth. Thinking that made me sad on account I didn't get a good chance to tell her that I'd be gone for a while. That was because her ma had been with her the last time I saw her, along with that scoundrel from Topeka, Mr. Louis Friedman, the special correspondent for *The Sporting News* and *Variety* who, iffen you was to ask me, just prostituted hisself by writing for any publication that would pay him. Though I'd never say that word—*prostituted*—whilst in earshot of Ruth.

Buckskin noticed how sad I got to looking. I think he figured out why I was so blue, so he took me to the City Drug Store, where he bought me some Purity Ice Cream. Remembering what had happened with them Valley Boys, I ate real slow.

"I was joking about shooting cowboys, kid," he said as we were sitting there. I stared at him. "Norris was standing behind you . . . so that comment was for his ears. Just a reminder."

Which didn't make me feel no better 'cause that reminded me of them two men Buckskin had shot dead. No, that ain't right. He'd kilt four men, at least, because I'd seen him shoot down Charles Gallagher in Axtell, and I also believed he might've drilled Thomas Gallagher that day, too.

"Well," I made myself say, "thanks for getting me out of Kansas."

Buckskin wolfed down his ice cream. "I did have ulterior motives."

I said: "Ulterior?"

He said: "Clandestine."

I said: "Clandestine?"

He smiled. "Hidden. Secret."

After taking another bite of ice cream, I asked: "What do you mean?" Figured Buckskin wouldn't tell me 'cause if I knew, then his motives wouldn't be clandestine, but I was glad when he did.

"I'm guessing it'll take Ed a while to find somebody in western Kansas willing to play baseball wearing bloomers and a topper. So the girls will get more experience playing baseball against men, which is what they want."

The ice cream started giving me a headache, but Buckskin told me to rub my tongue against the roof of my mouth. As I did that, he told me that this ice cream parlor was once one of the most notorious saloons in Dodge City.

"I think I'd make a good coach," Buckskin said, more like he was thinking aloud. "But going out like this gives me experience in organizing things. Booking games and hotels. Making sure we can get from one town to another.

And . . ."—he lowered his voice—"remember Emporia."

Thinking back to that town, I recollected Buckskin steering me into that alley there as those two cowboys passed through town and then taking me along while he bought cartridges for his big rifle.

"We'll be gone a month," Buckskin said, "so maybe that DeFee woman will figure you're not with the Bloomer Girls and she'll give up following the team. And the Kelton brothers will go back to Wyoming."

"Who are the Kelton brothers?" I asked, never having heard Buckskin mention that name before.

"Cousins of the two men I shot dead in Wyoming."

If that was supposed to make me feel better, it didn't, 'cause now I knew who those two cowboys back in Emporia had been. *If the Widow Amy DeFee or the Kelton brothers figure we ain't in Kansas,* I thought, *maybe they'll look for us in Colorado.*

I didn't say that aloud.

Maybe I should have.

Chapter Eighteen

Part of the team only were girls, but they put up a very good game, and the time honored saying that a girl can't throw straight, was exploded as they sent the ball in straight and swift.

Las Animas Leader
Las Animas, Colorado
July 27, 1906

Buckskin and me got to Colorado just fine, though at first it wasn't no cooler than Kansas, but at length we reached what they called the Front Range, and didn't sweat much after that. Over the next few weeks, Buckskin left me to be a ringer for some team whilst he traipsed across the plains, that weren't that much different than parts of Kansas, and the mountains, which were a lot different than anything I'd seen in Kansas, unless it was a drawing in *Harper's Weekly*. Buckskin said he let me play with town-ball teams so that my arm and swing wouldn't go bad, and that worried me. I don't mean I was concerned about my throwing and hitting getting no worser 'cause I'd been in slumps before and

Buckskin had taught me that I just had to ride them days out. But I feared that Buckskin might not come back iffen the Kelton boys caught up with him.

Or that the Widow Amy DeFee and Kevin Brett, that villainous judge, might catch up to me whilst I didn't have no pard with an 1886 Winchester repeater in .45-90 caliber and a .38-caliber double-action Colt to protect me, which is kind of selfish thinking, but Buckskin keeps telling me to stay honest in this here narrative.

Buckskin, though, he come back to Pueblo and Trinidad, and took me with him to some other cities. He had games scheduled for Breckenridge, Cañon City, Castle Rock, Denver, Fort Collins, La Junta, Lamar, Las Animas, Rocky Ford, Salida, and Trinidad—that being alphabetical order and not the order we played the games. Buckskin had challenged me to list the teams by the alphabet and says, after I let him see what I written down, that I done real, real fine.

Them Colorado mountains are mighty pretty, and when we got to Leadville, which didn't have no team for us to play, Buckskin made me pitch and bat and throw and catch with him, which plumb near kilt me and caused my nose to bleed and my chest to heave. He said I needed to get used to being up the mountains, and whilst I'd always liked Buckskin and thought he liked me, I began to suspicion that maybe he was working for the Widow Amy DeFee and this was her way of torturing me before she had me killed. But once my nose stopped bleeding and after I stopped getting sicker than a mad dog from running to the graveyard and back, I come to feel pretty good. I think, too, it helped that I slept good, 'cause for me them mountains brought on sleep just like a train could, even without the clickety-clacking-go-to-sleep sounds.

"Are you going to work Ruth, Cassie, and Maggie this hard?" I asked him.

"I won't be managing the Bloomers then," he said, "and you know Norris doesn't care if they win. All he cares about is making money."

We left Leadville and headed south to Pueblo, and Buckskin left me there to play for the Lithia Ball Club, which got its name from its sponsor, Lithia Water Bottling Company, meaning I had to work for the company since Mr. Norris wasn't paying me to travel with Buckskin and hide out from the Widow Amy DeFee and those Kelton brothers. It weren't much fun filling bottles with water from the Colorado Lithia Well, which was some twelve hundred feet deep, but I knew the widow and judge wouldn't look for me there, and whilst the baseball team wasn't very good it was the only team I knew that could spell its name—L-I-T-H-I-A—with baseball bats lined up on the ground. Which tells you something about how people in Pueblo entertain themselves.

When Buckskin fetched me in Trinidad——
where I played after Pueblo—he said that had he
known how easy it was to schedule ball games,
he'd have taken up this job a whole lot sooner.
Folks wanted to play the Bloomer Girls in
Colorado as much as they wanted to in Kansas.

Buckskin had got all the games we needed, and
I felt fine because I'd been swinging the bat real
good. Buckskin and me shot some billiards and
ate some mountain oysters which didn't taste
like snot, before we left Trinidad and went to Las
Animas, where there weren't no mountains and
where they warned us to look out for rattlesnakes
in the outfield.

Whilst we was waiting at the depot for the train
that would bring the Bloomer Girls to Colorado
for our first game, my stomach was filled with
butterflies on account I was so nervous to see
beautiful, sweet Ruth. Buckskin was reading
a newspaper from a bunch he had collected
on trains. He called me over and showed me
The Nortonville News which got published in
Nortonville, Kansas, a town I'd never heard of.

Thus I read this:

> Snail Snyder, the Effingham ball player
> who was invited to leave Effingham
> because of a robbery in that city, has again
> been heard of. He is playing ball with the
> Bloomer girls.

Weeks earlier, Buckskin had showed me the telegraph that Mr. Norris had sent Buckskin in Colorado Springs that said Charlie Barngrover had joined the Bloomers and was pitching for them instead of Russ Waddell, who was recovering from having a copper tube shoved up his . . . well, I don't want to write that down or remember it 'cause it makes me practically double over in pain just thinking about it.

"It don't say what position he plays," I said.

Which scared me that if I got scratched from the Bloomer Girls, I'd have to pedal my Hawthorne over Raton Pass and into New Mexico and keep on pedaling all the way till I got to Mexico. I spoke neither Mexican nor New Mexican.

"He's not releasing you or me," Buckskin said.

"How do you know?"

"Because I scare the sunshine out of Ed." At this point, you know that Buckskin did not say *sunshine*.

"I don't cotton to the notion of having a robber for a teammate," I said. I already had to deal with Louis Friedman, who did not steal, as far as I knew, but who I did not like on account he took up too much time with Ruth.

"We'll keep an eye on him," Buckskin said.

Five minutes later, the train whistle blew, so Buckskin and me rose from that uncomfortable bench, and stepped out onto the platform. My heart started pounding when I saw the black

202

smoke pouring out of the stack as the train got closer, bringing Ruth so much closer to my heart.

Eighteen of Methuselah's lifetimes passed before that smoking, squeaking, ringing, grunting, whistling locomotive come to a stop. Buckskin and me waited as the porter ran around, a mama and a baby got off and was greeted by a *vaquero*—whatever that is— in a black hat and with silver buttons running up both sides of his pants. I'd never seen pants that had to be buttoned on the sides as well as where buttons usually go on britches. Then the boxcar was opened, and our crew began taking out our equipment, which meant that this was the right train.

Next thing I knew, Maggie Casey was leaping down from the train, not even taking the porter's offer of his big hand, not even acknowledging the fellow. She turned around and bellowed: "Come on, Bloomers, let's see if the whiskey and men here are any better than they was the last time we visited!" This sounded more like something Nelse McConnell would've said, only he would've substituted *men* for a word much more impolite than *women*.

Carrie Cassady climbed down next, but she let the porter help her. When she saw Buckskin and me, she smiled and waved happily. Buckskin and me waved back as other Bloomer Girls got out. My heart just sank when Mrs. Eagan stepped onto the platform, and brought out a fan that she unfolded and started fanning herself on account that it was hot and dusty in Las Animas.

It should not have affected me that way because I knew that Ruth would not have come to Colorado without her ma, so I recovered right quick because beautiful Ruth stepped off the train next.

I smiled.

Till my heart broke into a million pieces.

For the next person who climbed down from the car wasn't no Bloomer Girl but Louis Friedman, the correspondent for *The Sporting News*, *Variety*, and any other publication that would pay him to write. He had the audacity to take Ruth's arm and escort her away from Maggie Casey, who was barking orders at the other Bloomer Girls and telling Carrie Cassady to stop acting like a child by waving at strangers. Carrie Cassady said something too soft for us to hear over the screeching, clanging, and grunting of the engine, and the screaming of the baby that belonged to the mama and the *vaquero*. So maybe you see why my heart smashed into little pieces.

Maggie Casey turned around and saw us, and then she raised her hand, but it wasn't no friendly wave as it was the back of her hand that she let us see, along with her lowered thumb and every finger but the middle one, which ain't a polite kind of wave but was something ballists often done to an umpire after a terrible call as long as the umpire wasn't looking. I'd done that, too, but to a pitcher who threw a fastball too close to my head.

Mrs. Eagan walked alongside Ruth. Louis Friedman stopped to shake our hands. Buckskin told them where the hotel was, and Ruth looked at me and smiled and said: "It's nice to see you again." But she didn't say my name, neither Lucy Totton nor my real name, and Mrs. Eagan asked if it was always this dusty in Las Animas. Buckskin shrugged, and the hacks started arriving, so Ruth and her ma and that ink-slinging rapscallion—picked up that word my ownself from *The Adventures of Huckleberry Finn*—and got a ride to the hotel.

At length, Mr. Ed Norris emerged from the train with two strangers who were decked out in toppers and Bloomer Girls duds. We greeted Mr. Norris and Snail Snyder, who wasn't no bigger than me but had eyes real close together above his crooked nose, and Charlie Barngrover, who smelt like a busted whiskey keg. He had trouble keeping his balance when Buckskin and me reached out to shake his hand.

CHAPTER NINETEEN

The La Junta team kicked and the blooming girls picked up their dolls and things and announced that they were going back home and would never speak to the La Junta boys again as long as they lived.

La Junta Tribune
La Junta, Colorado
July 25, 1906

Buckskin looked at Mr. Norris and asked: "Where's Nelse?"

"Where do you think?" he answered, which wasn't an answer.

Buckskin give our manager one of them looks. "He's in jail?" Buck said next.

The little weasel named Snail smirked. "Instead of bustin' up a saloon, he busted up the Palace Drug Store. Picked up a Spaldin' bat they was sellin' and went loco. Ruint every croquet set they had in the store. Then he went to work on the laxatives, the aspirin, soda pops, and the telephone."

"You didn't bail him out?" Buckskin said.

"No bail," our manager said. "Not after he broke a policeman's arm with that bat."

"Your ex-catcher must like coppers as much as he likes croquet," the weasel said, sniggering.

Charlie Barngrover, who needed a shave if he wanted to pass for a Bloomer Girl, threw hisself into the conversation. "It's a meaningless sport."

Buckskin and Mr. Norris paid them no mind. The latter said: "Your West isn't so wild anymore. By Jehovah, in Dodge they're making residents put tags on their dogs these days. Charge a dollar a year."

Making no comment about Dodge City's dogs or nothing else, Buckskin handed what he called "our Colorado itinerary" to Mr. Norris, who studied it after spitting out his cigar onto the platform.

He nodded after reading it over and said: "One thing's missing."

Buckskin waited.

"Who runs the gambling in these towns?"

Buckskin didn't answer, said instead: "Without Nelse, who's your catcher? I don't think it's this runt."

"Who you callin' a runt?" the weasel said.

Buckskin gave Snail a mean stare. "Would you prefer robber?"

"He wasn't convicted, Buck," Mr. Norris said.

Charlie Barngrover laughed. " 'Cause he busted out of what Effingham calls a jail."

Mr. Norris took charge, which ain't nothing he done regular, but I was glad because it likely stopped some fisticuffs from erupting at the depot. I was already missing Waddell and Nelse, especially 'cause we had booked a room at a hotel that had Buckskin, me, the weasel and the drunk sharing a room.

"Let's find the hotel," the weasel said. "I'm hungry."

"Try the oysters," Buckskin told him.

Buckskin had to catch the game against Las Animas and La Junta, and I had to pitch both on account that Charlie Barngrover was in his cups. No, *in his cups* doesn't quite draw the right picture. Some of the boys who put up our canvas fences and the grandstand had to haul Charlie Barngrover in a wheelbarrow from the ballpark to the depot. See, Mr. Norris done all he could to keep any liquor out of our new Lady Waddell's reach, but Charlie Barngrover outsmarted him.

We lost them games against Las Animas . . . La Junta . . . Lamar.

Dark times.

Ruth spent so much time with Louis Friedman and her ma, I hardly got a chance to talk to her, and really only saw her when I'd be pitching and have to check the runner on first base. To make up for my lack of contact with her, I'd make quite a few throws to her at first, never coming close to getting the base-runner out, and wearing out Ruth's $4 Spalding mitt, till the spectators started yelling obscenities at me to throw to the batter and quit stalling.

Darkest of times.

"Do you know what wins more ball games than anything else?" Buckskin asked me as we rode the train to Trinidad. They'd left Charlie Barngrover, by the way, in the boxcar with the benches, grandstand, fences, and other equipment, so he could sleep off his bender.

"Scoring runs," I said, which we hadn't been doing much of since the Bloomer Girls come to Colorado.

Buckskin grinned but shook his head. "It's how the players get along . . . how they work together."

Which made me feel blue way down in my heart and soul 'cause way back in Kansas I had gotten along real fine with kind, pretty Ruth. Now Maggie Casey talked to me more than Ruth, and what Maggie said wasn't always friendly.

"You reckon it's us?" I asked. "The girls were doing real good in Kansas."

"No," Buckskin said.

"Charlie and Snail?"

He shook his head.

"We wasn't with the team for a whole month," I said. "Maybe something happened." That sent the blood rushing to my head and caused me to ball my fingers till my fists shook and my knuckles turned white. Me thinking that the something was Louis Friedman.

But Buckskin didn't mention that ink-slinger. He called our manager into question. "Ed's up to something," Buckskin said.

Which sort of disappointed me as I'd been imagining sending a pitch so wild that Buckskin wouldn't be able to catch it before it hit Louis Friedman in his lips and teeth and nose and then went through his face like Buckskin's .45-90 bullet had gone through Charles Gallagher's chest back in Axtell, Kansas.

"Could be the attitude," I suggested after my anger died down. "Though I ain't seen none of the girls suffering from a bleeding nose."

Buckskin give me a curious look. "*A*ltitude," he finally said. "Not attitude."

I shrugged.

"Do you think Ed's been acting a little strange, kid?"

Another shrug.

"When a team loses, it's the manager who gets the blame," Buckskin muttered to himself.

"Or the umpire," I added.

"Ed's up to something," Buckskin said.

"So's Friedman," I whispered.

"What?" Buckskin said.

"Nothing."

Buckskin pondered more. I devised plans

that would result in painful injuries for Louis Friedman till the noise of the train moving in the night put me to sleep.

It was Denver where Maggie Casey got fed up. Buckskin had been catching every game, and that was all right for a ballist like Nelse McConnell, who didn't know no better because he was stupid and couldn't play no position but catcher. But Buckskin was a thinker and a planner and, usually, a third baseman—and, yeah, a killer and a crack shot and a reader of anything with words—but Mr. Norris wouldn't give him a break. Me, neither. I pitched every game, and Buckskin, in his topper and a catcher's mitt that didn't really fit him, catched every game.

Till Maggie Casey got into Mr. Norris's face right before our game in Denver, and she called our manager all sorts of bad things, saying he was a disgrace, and that if he didn't let Carrie Cassady pitch against the Bears and have Maud Nelson catch, Mr. Ed Norris would rue the day.

That got Charlie Barngrover to laughing, but he stopped when Maggie Casey snatched the glove off his lap and pulled out all the little bottles of whiskey that he'd been hiding inside his mitt. Charlie's face turned whiter than fresh snow on the highest peak in the Colorado Rockies, and then turned redder than a plate of beets— which are disgusting and should never be served nowhere—when Maggie ripped open his shirt and grabbed his unmentionables and plucked out two large grapefruits that he had stuffed in there so he'd look more like a girl than a drunk ballist.

Maggie Casey tossed one of the grapefruits to Katie Maloney and another to Gypsie O'Hearn as she said: "See if those taste like gin, girls."

Charlie Barngrover's mouth hung open as he sucked in a deep, deep breath—not because he wasn't used to the a/titude but because Maggie Casey had found out where he hid his gin and rye and bourbon and corn liquor and bitters.

"You'll find a syringe in his shaving kit," Maggie said. "He puts liquor in fruit . . . grapefruit, lemons, oranges . . . whatever he can find. When he can't find fruit, he juices up his tobacco plugs."

Which led me to wonder how come he could swallow his liquor but not the tobacco juice. That stuff had made me sicker than a dog when I tried it when I was twelve, playing with a bunch of farm boys. One of them boys said he had learnt how to swallow tobacco juice without getting sick, but he never told me the secret to it. But that was fine, 'cause I never wanted to stick that grossness into my mouth again.

Maggie put a long finger underneath Barngrover's nose. "If I ever smell liquor on your breath again, buster, I'll rip off your head and spit down the hole."

Barngrover disappeared quick after the game in Denver. Didn't say good bye or draw his time. Nobody missed him much, and Maggie banned any kind of fruit that people could suck on at our bench.

Buckskin and me didn't play in the Denver game. The Bloomer Girls didn't win, but they played good.

Buckskin whispered to me: "Remember this day, kid. This is the day when the Bloomer Girls' luck turned."

CHAPTER TWENTY

It is truly marvelous how skill-
fully these girls can handle a
base ball while the pitching
of Miss Carrie Cassady, who
is a left handed wonder, is
remarkable. She has been named
Lady Waddell after the famous
south paw of the Philadelphia
American base ball club and is
the best lady ball player on
earth. All of the fans in the
city and especially the ladies
and children should turn out and
see this wonderful team of lady
artists play the great national
game.

Whitehorn News
Whitehorn, Colorado
July 20, 1906

The Bloomer Girls started winning, and after
Snail Snyder got hisself arrested for robbing
the Pike's Peak Poultry Yards—never found out
if he was stealing eggs or Rose Comb Rhode
Island Reds. Still, folks and the law take their

birds and yokes serious in Colorado Springs and since the weasel had stole Buckskin's double-action Colt to commit the crime, the law and the judge, who prided hisself on his winter layers and good roasters, wasn't inclined to give Snail no bail since the Bloomers were leaving Colorado Springs and wouldn't be in the state of Colorado for long. Mr. Norris didn't have much choice but to play mostly girls, though I pitched every third day when Buckskin usually catched.

The lineup was usually this: Carrie Cassady or Gypsie O'Hearn pitched. Maggie Casey, Pearl Murphy, and Katie Maloney in the outfield. Sue Malarkey at second and Agnes McGuire at shortstop. Maude Sullivan and Ruth Eagan at the corners. Maud Nelson, who wasn't a bad pitcher at all and could play practically anywhere on the field, and Jessie Dailey played when they weren't selling programs or tickets.

They got good, our girls, didn't get tired out from the altitude, and Carrie Cassady had a spitball that was impossible to hit, even though it ain't lady-like for even Quaker girls from Salem, Ohio, to spit.

Once, when it wasn't the third day, meaning I didn't have to pitch, I asked Mr. Norris if he'd like me to sell programs or tickets. He pulled out his cigar, squinted his eyes, and said: "You ain't that pretty, bub." Which was truthful, if rude. I didn't bother to ask him if he'd want Buckskin to give one of the Bloomer Girls a rest from hawking programs because while I ain't as pretty as that sweet waitress in Salida, I look better than Buckskin Compton, and he cuts a much finer figure than Mr. Norris.

Colorado's mountains were beautiful. We ate a mess of trout, which tasted great. Not one nose on any of the Bloomer Girls bled, and in the mountains, unlike on the plains, nary a single Coloradan refused to pay the two-bits to watch our games. They wanted to see the Bloomers play, and usually, excepting on them third days when Buckskin and me played, they actually seen girls play baseball against men.

Buckskin and me were having breakfast before taking the rented wagons to Whitehorn, which didn't have no train. I'd ordered trout and eggs, though I'd never tried fish for breakfast before, but it was sure good for supper. The waitress, who was prettier than Ruth, smiled and said that was what she liked for breakfast, too. I grinned, and she said she had been to the baseball game the day before. And I said that I had, too, praying silently that she had not seen me on the bench decked out like a female.

"Don't you love the geese?" she asked.

I nodded. "I've never played a game where geese . . ." Only I shut up because I didn't want

216

her to know that I could have played in that game dressed up as a Bloomer Girl.

"You play baseball?" She asked that like some people would say: *You own a gold mine?*

I shrugged. "Second base. Some pitching. Anywhere."

She didn't bring up the geese again, so I'll explain that in Salida, Colorado, geese often rest themselves in the outfield, center field mostly, but it depends on the shade. And no visiting team nor the Salida Nine is allowed to harm no geese, or even try to shoo them big birds out of the playing area. They're just a part of the ground rules that the umpire told everybody before the game. But if you know anything about a goose, you already know that only a fool would try to herd a goose or two from anywhere because geese is mean, fierce birds that'll attack anyone. Folks here in Salida come to see the games in the summer and fall, hoping that a ball will drop in the outfield and get them geese madder than ganders. They enjoy watching an outfielder try to get the ball and throw it in without getting pecked or crapped on.

Maggie Casey wasn't eating breakfast that morning 'cause she'd agitated a mama goose in center field and got her throwing hand scratched up bad. The Salidans at the game had sure loved that. Made me and Buckskin chuckle, but not once Maggie Casey run in after the inning, cussing and screaming, and forcing me and Maud Nelson to find a clean cloth to put over her bleeding hand.

"We have a good team," the red-headed waitress said, "but need a new manager and captain."

"Is that so?" Buckskin decided to put hisself into my conversation with this nice, young, red-headed waitress. Ruth's hair didn't have even a hint of red.

"Yeah." It wasn't the red-headed waitress who said that, but a big miner sitting at the counter next to a coffee-slurping cowboy, who also decided to put hisself into my talk with the waitress. The cowboy nudged the man in the pin-striped suit next to him, and that fellow turned around and grinned.

"Lynched the little . . . ," the cowboy started to say.

But it was the man in the pin stripes who finished the cowboy's sentence, calling the manager a word that caused the red-headed waitress to blush.

Then the miner said: "You best not try to rob any store in our town, boys."

The waitress come to our defense, saying: "They don't plan to do that, Zane."

The fellow in pin stripes opened his mouth to say something, but the waitress said: "Keep your trap shut, Max, and finish your coffee."

The cowboy slurped more coffee, the redhead give me a pitiful look and apologized for Zane's and Max's rudeness, but did say she sure wished the Salida Nine could find a new manager.

That's when the bell above the door jingled, and Louis Friedman stepped in and stood, beckoning the red-headed waitress over. I heard him tell her there'd be two ladies joining him in ten minutes. I hoped them fish and eggs would come soon, though I doubted I could wolf down my breakfast in ten minutes. More and more folks began piling into the café, so I didn't get much more time to talk to the red-headed waitress except to thank her when I paid for my meal. As I followed Buckskin out, I nodded at Ruth and her ma, who sat in a corner booth.

Mr. Norris took the stagecoach to Whitehorn, and back, too, after we played the Miners, who was really miners and not just the name they gave the team. Buckskin said I might have to take over pitching, as we were at an altitude of more than nine thousand feet.

Gypsie O'Hearn did good and pitched the whole game. We won, and then returned to Salida in our rented wagons. I wanted to have more trout and eggs for breakfast, but the café was closed, it being Sunday, so I just had coffee at this hut beside the depot before we took the Denver & Rio Grande to Cañon City, which is where Snail

Snyder was going to be spending a year just for trying to steal chickens with a .38-caliber pistol.

We beat Cañon City, too, and went on to Pueblo, where we bottled up Lithia. Buckskin said I had made a good pun when I read that line to him, even though I didn't know what a pun was, but I knew that we had beat Pueblo's team 4-to-0.

We kept winning ball games but then took a train to Greeley, where all our luck went to Hades.

CHAPTER TWENTY-ONE

Ed Morris, manager of the National Bloomer Girls' base ball team of Kansas City, skipped out Thursday morning for parts unknown, leaving the girls behind. However, [this] fact did not disturb the girls in the least, as he had no hold on the company pocketbook. One of their number, already financial manager, stepped into the shoes of the general manager, and the game went on.

The Greeley Tribune
Greeley, Colorado
August 2, 1906

Ed Norris . . ."—Buckskin paused as we stood at the front desk at the hotel in Greeley—"checked out?"

It had been a long train ride from Pueblo.

"He never checked in, sir," the pock-marked fellow with the brass-frame spectacles told us.

"He must have been delayed," Buckskin said, looking like he was thinking hard. He glanced at me, glanced out the big, front window behind him, and turned back to give the clerk a confident smile. But when Buckskin looked at me, I didn't see no confidence at all. Just a troubled, worried, even petrified ballist. Yet when Buckskin faced the clerk again, he made himself sound like everything was going like it was supposed to be going.

"But you have all of the rooms for the Bloomer Girls in order?" Buckskin inquired.

"Of course."

"Good, good, sir." He kept his tone friendly, upbeat, and even his eyes didn't have no uneasy look to them if you didn't know him. But to me, Buckskin's eyes revealed that he was ready to rip off somebody's head and spit down the hole. Luckily that head wasn't mine or the fellow who was turning the register around so that Buckskin could sign it.

"Thank you," Buckskin said. "The girls will be checking in directly."

"Excellent. Including Lucy Totton?"

Hearing my Bloomer Girl name, Buckskin looked at me. I wasn't dressed as no Bloomer Girl, though I was supposed to be. Buckskin had said that was foolish these days and unless Mr. Norris insisted, I shouldn't dress up except when we was at the ballpark. When I had reminded him that I had the Widow Amy DeFee to worry about, he nodded, sighed, and left it up to me. So I decided that unless I was at a Bloomer

Girls' game, I wouldn't wear no bloomers or no dresses, but it would be my own fault if I got kilt for dressing up in that suit I'd bought in Kansas.

"What do you want with Lucy?" Buckskin asked the clerk.

"Oh, nothing," the clerk said. "We just have read so much about her." He looked at the door. "We've heard about all the Bloomer Girls. The whole town will be on hand for the game tomorrow."

"Good," Buckskin said. "Lucy Totton's a great player."

"Yes, she is."

"So is Francis Marion," Buckskin said.

"Indeed," said the clerk.

"And Blair Baddeley."

"Yes, yes. Your team is loaded with exceptional ladies. I sure hope many of those girls will honor me with their autographs."

"As soon as they check in," Buckskin said. "Thank you. Most are still at the depot gathering their bags." He rubbed his chin, which needed a shave, but it didn't matter 'cause he wasn't dressed in his Bloomer uniform, neither. "Is the telegraph office open?"

"At this hour?" The clerk looked apologetic. "I'm afraid it wouldn't be."

Buckskin glanced at the telephone that hung on the wall. He considered the staircase, the elevator, the newspapers piled on one corner of the desk, our grips that we'd put on the floor next to us. We had got to the hotel ahead of the Bloomer Girls 'cause Mr. Norris had left Buckskin in charge after catching an early train to Greeley, and not because it takes girls longer to gather their things together.

At length, Buckskin said: "Might we leave our luggage here until everyone is checked in?"

The clerk looked happy 'cause now he had something to do, but when he looked at the big clock on the mantel of the stone fireplace, he said: "I will be off duty in fifteen minutes, but I can have Jorge take your cases and bags up to your room . . . Mister . . . ?"

"Madison," Buckskin said. "Dole E. Madison." When he'd booked the hotel weeks ago, he'd put his Bloomer Girl alias down since he figured that Mr. Norris would be back to taking care of the business end of things.

The clerk looked confused as he studied his list of reservations, but Buckskin didn't give him a chance to think much about it, saying: "If you have me down as Dolly, don't fret. It happens all the time." As he said this, he fished a coin from his pocket and slid it across the cherry-wood counter top, which the clerk took discreetly, nodding solemnly. Buckskin picked up his bat bag that held only the Winchester .45-90 since the Colt revolver had been confiscated by the law after they'd arrested Snail Snyder in Colorado Springs.

"Would you like Jorge to take that bag up as well?" the clerk asked.

"No, but thank you. I might need this." Buckskin turned to me. "And you should take your grip, too." He pointed to one of my bags, but I didn't have no weapon in it. "In case you run into Francis."

I didn't know no Francis, and knew nobody played for the Bloomer Girls with that handle, but I did just like Buckskin told me to do. He thanked the clerk again and give me a nod that told me to follow him.

"Something's not right," he told me once we were outside and he was leaning against the wall of the hotel in an alley where there was hardly no light at all shining on us.

I asked: "Is Francis Marion replacing Charlie Barngrover or Snail Snyder?"

"Francis Marion was a hero of the Revolutionary War."

Then he'd be far too old to help us, I thought to myself.

"And who's this Blair Baddeley you mentioned?" I asked as I set my grip on the dirt.

"Another one of my aliases," he said, removing his hat and running his hands through his hair. He didn't say nothing else, just adjusted how he was carrying his bag, before heading down the alley. He didn't stop till he found the privies, though he and me both had gone when we got off the train. He opened a door and told me to get in.

"Change into your Bloomer uniform," he ordered, before I could protest, not sounding like my bunkie or pard no more, but my manager, my coach, my boss.

"Wait fifteen minutes. The new clerk should be on duty by then. Sign in as Lady Waddell. Not Lucy Totton. Lady Waddell. You got that? Lady Waddell."

I got it. Buckskin never said nothing three times, so I knew he was serious.

"When you get into the room, wedge a chair under the doorknob, and don't let anyone in till you hear my voice. *Not a soul.* Savvy?"

I didn't, but said I did. Standing in the two-seater, Buckskin let go of the door, and it slammed shut. I had just started to change when there was a pounding on the rickety door.

"Kid," Buckskin called. "Forget what I said about the hotel. Do *not* go back to that hotel. If somebody asked about Lucy Totton, there's only one person that can be, and that's your stepmother."

Almost messed my britches.

"Get dressed. Meet me back at the depot. Savvy?"

A squeak of a word left my lips.

Didn't hear nothing after that but Buckskin's footsteps.

A darkened outhouse, even a four-seater, in a strange city ain't the best place for a fellow to change into bloomers and a girls blouse, but I done my best, then I waited until the fellow in the two-seater privy, immediately behind mine, was done. I pray I never eat whatever it was that afflicted him, but as soon as I heard him leave, I edged open the door, made sure nobody was waiting to answer Nature's call, and then I got my bag, straightened my cap, and moved down that alley.

Screams commenced to cut through the night, and they were coming from the depot. Since Greeley had gas street lamps, I could see folks running around, and most were wearing Bloomer uniforms. And there was no mistaking Maggie Casey's bass notes.

"Ruth . . . Ruth . . . Carrie . . . Carrie . . . !"

"Ruth? Have you seen Ruth?"

"Carrie . . . Carrie . . . where are you?"

I sprinted back to the depot, where a figure rushed out of an alley, and grabbed my shoulder and spun me around.

"Have you seen Ruth?" Louis Friedman asked, fright filling his wide eyes. He shook me so hard that my bag slipped to the dirt as he shouted in my face: "Where is she?"

My right arm came up to knock both of his

227

hands away, and I told him that I didn't know were Ruth was.

"Carrie? Carrie? Where are you?" That's what Pearl Murphy was shouting. I didn't know where she was, neither.

"My baby . . . my baby . . ."

Even Mrs. Eagan's sobs sort of pained my heart, and I didn't like Mrs. Eagan, never had. Besides, I was becoming more than a little annoyed over the I'm-so-pretty-and-you-ain't-nothing-other-than-a-boy-playing-a-girl game Ruth had been playing since she and the others had joined Buckskin and me in Colorado.

Friedman staggered back, blinking rapidly. "Are you sure you haven't seen her?"

"I haven't seen her since I got off the train," I said.

"Where have you been? What have you been doing? Why haven't you been helping us look for her?"

I bit my bottom lip, and allowed him to keep spouting out questions since he was a writer—though just a correspondent and not a staff writer—for *The Sporting News*. When he finally stopped talking to draw hisself a breath, I said: "I was with Buckskin trying to check into the hotel."

He stopped, turned, looked down the street. "The hotel," he repeated, looking down the street, spun back toward me, and said: "Has she checked in?"

"No," I told him. "Buckskin and me were the first there."

It didn't occur to me until Friedman got distracted by a wagon and ran over to it, yelling at the driver, who stopped and appeared ready to take off Friedman's nose with his bullwhip, that it might be that Ruth, and Carrie, too, had checked into the hotel whilst I was in that privy getting into my Bloomer uniform, even though he didn't seem to care nothing about where Carrie had gotten herself to.

Louis Friedman continued to travel down the street, stopping people with questions. More and more people were gathering in the street, even some strangers, shouting out for Ruth and Carrie. When I spotted Buckskin off by some corrals, I grabbed my grip and ran toward him. But before I got halfway to him, he had left. I tried to call out to him, but with all the others yelling, my voice was probably drowned out. I hadn't quite caught up with him when he turned the corner and headed down another street. I found him looking at a trash bin that had been tipped over in front of The Goodman & Neill Clothing Company.

Hearing my footsteps, Buckskin turned as he reached toward his bat bag, but the street lamps must have shown him my face, so he knew it was me and not one of the Kelton brothers. He acknowledged me with a nod of his head, then bent to reach inside the trash bin.

Buckskin didn't say nothing, didn't ask nothing, for he didn't need to. He knew what it was and who it belonged to, same as me.

It was a BXS first baseman's mitt, from A.G. Spalding & Brothers, priced at $4. Practically brand new, I knew Ruth wouldn't have thrown it in no trash can. Not after the game she'd played in Pueblo.

Buckskin said: "Find a lawman."

Feeling sicker than liquor ever made Nelse McConnell or even Charlie Barngrover, I obeyed. I had almost reached the corner, when Buckskin called out my name and told me to stop. Which I done, and headed back.

"What is it?" I asked.

He was holding a piece of paper that he was reading in the dim light. When he was finished, he handed it to me.

Chapter Twenty-Two

This is a first class team and are known from coast to coast. The ladies travel in their own special car and make ball playing a business. Don't fail to see this game.

The Castle Rock Journal
Castle Rock, Colorado
July 13, 1906

W hat the farthing is going on?" Maggie Casey said, and she did say *farthing*. Might have been 'cause Louis Friedman was in the room and she generally talked nicer when the press was around, even though Friedman could hear Maggie cussing like a bullwhacker whilst he was covering our games.

"Exactly what the note says," Buckskin said before turning to me. "Right?"

Maggie had just finished reading the note that Buckskin had found, and now Louis Friedman was reading it.

I said: "It's her handwriting."

"Whose?" Maggie asked.

"The kid's mother's," Buckskin said.

"Stepma," I corrected. "Not my birthing ma."

231

"Lord have mercy," Louis Friedman said, which meant he read what the Widow Amy DeFee had put in the note that she had stuck inside Ruth's new mitt, and then in the trash can.

The note was handed back to me, but I didn't want it no more 'cause them words had done been burned inside my brain.

Here's what it said, though it's hard for me to replicate in my Daisy Writing Tablet 'cause the Widow Amy DeFee had cut out letters, numbers, and whole words from newspapers to make up this note, excepting for the last paragraph, which she wrote and which I recognized as being her handwriting.

My name come from the write-up about our game in Colorado Springs, but the fool reporter for *The Weekly Gazette* had spelled my name wrong—it's *o-n*, not *e-n*—though it ain't my real name, so it don't matter.

Lucy Totten

You & U alone will br*ing*
$5,000
To FoRt VaSquEz tomorrow
after the team Leaves *4*
Breckenridge
Or the 2 *girls*
DIE
Lucy's Pal will *bring*

$5000 to the game in
Breckenridge
WHICH
U will los*e*
oR the *2* girls
DIE
Lucy comes al<u>o</u>Ne
Don't get the Law
Involved
Or *the* <u>GIRLS</u> diE

The written part in the Widow Amy DeFee's own hand said:

Ask young Lucy if I mean what I say. Follow my instructions to the letter. The girls will be returned, unharmed, after you lose Tuesday's game. I will find you in the grandstand in Breckenridge. Or ELSE!

"What's this all about?" Louis Friedman asked.

Buckskin nodded at me. I sighed, and after telling the ink-slinger about the widow, the evil judge, me, my pa, and how I come to hide out with a women's baseball team, Louis Friedman gave me and Buckskin a dumb look. His lips parted every few seconds, but he, who made his living writing words, couldn't find nothing to say, so he reread the note.

"Why does she want the Bloomers to lose to Breckenridge?" he finally said.

"If you knew the Widow Amy DeFee like I do, you'd know she and that murdering Judge Brett has bet a tidy sum on Breckenridge," I told him. Which would've been a sure bet back in the olden times when the girls was losing and Lady Waddell was suffering from what folks call an indelicate affliction and Nelse McConnell was drunk, but not these times, now that the Bloomers kept winning. It also explained why they had kidnapped Carrie Cassady, who was pitching great, and Ruth Eagan, who had become not only a first-rate first basewoman but good at some timely hits.

Friedman pondered what I'd said a while, causing his forehead to get all scrunched up and his hands to ball into fists because he had learnt what I'd known for the longest time: the Widow Amy DeFee is vile, repulsive, mean, contemptible, and one poor excuse for a woman. She had kidnapped two innocent young ladies, still in their teens, who had never harmed nobody except by lowering their batting averages, and now that evil harlot was holding those young ladies for a mighty big ransom. Plus, she had bet on a baseball game, bet for Breckenridge to win, for she knew we'd have to lose to save the innocent girls' lives—not that we had much of a chance to win without them—and that didn't even include the fact that my stepma was making me deliver half of that ransom money to some place called Fort Vasquez.

"Five thousand dollars." Friedman's head shook.

"Ten thousand," Buckskin corrected. "Five thousand to be taken to Fort Vasquez, and five thousand to be left at the game at Breckenridge."

"That's a lot of money."

"Carrie and Ruth are worth it," I said soberly.

The ink-slinger blinked, swallowed, and shook his head. "I mean . . . can Ed Norris come up with that much cash?"

Buckskin sighed long and hard. "That's another problem. Norris lit a shuck. With the cashbox."

Friedman got another dumb look on his face. "What exactly does this Western colloquialism . . . 'lit a shuck' . . . mean?"

Later, Buckskin told me that Friedman had been in shock, which explained the dumb looks and stupid questions, and I guess that might be expected. Besides, I admit that I felt pretty good when I told the writer that *lit a shuck* come about because folks lit corn shucks to find their way home, or wherever they was off to, when it had grown dark, and had become a saying used when someone took off in a hurry, often in the dead of night. You knew them kind of things when you grew up in Kansas, of course, unless you was an ignorant writer in Topeka.

"I can get ten thousand dollars," Friedman said, "but not by tomorrow. Tomorrow's Sunday. The banks are closed." He paused before asking: "After the game, our receipts will add up to . . . ?"

Buckskin's head started shaking. "Won't be near that much, even on our best day." He let out another weary breath. "And the crew wants to be paid . . ." He paused in deep thought, cocking his head the way smart folks do when they're contemplating an idea, and finally said: "Greeley's manager was interested in our grandstand and canvas fences."

"You mean sell it to them?" Friedman asked.

"Yeah," Buckskin said. "But there's still the problem of the banks being closed on Sundays. Plus, I arranged a special train to get us to Breckenridge. It's not a normal stop for the Colorado and Southern line. They're going to want their money, too, and so will our hotel."

"Write a check," Louis Friedman said. "When it doesn't . . ."

"Mister . . ."—Buckskin's tone got stern—"Western men have this little thing called honesty."

Mr. Friedman opened his mouth, but no words come out. Me, I was thinking that Judge Brett and Snail Snyder was Western men, too, and neither of them possessed nothing near honesty.

Buckskin sighed.

"I have enough to cover the checks . . . for

both the hotel and the special train. Count on it," said Mr. Friedman. Then he asked the obvious question most folks would ask: "Shouldn't we go to the Greeley police and tell . . . ?"

"No, absolutely not," Buckskin said, not even letting Friedman finish his sentence. "If word of this got out, it would be bad for the team . . . maybe for all female teams. There's enough people already say the sport is too dangerous for girls. Can you imagine what they would say if they heard that two of our players had been kidnapped and a ransom demanded. A lot of parents would stop letting their daughters get anywhere near a baseball field, much less play the sport. So, no . . . that's not an option. Besides, based on what the kid's told me about these two . . . well, I don't even want to think about it."

The journalist's face whitened. "What shall we do?" he asked.

Buckskin looked more tired than I'd ever seen him, even when he was catching a game when I couldn't do nothing but spike fastballs a foot in front of the plate. We sat in silence.

Finally, Buckskin told us the best plan he could come up with, even though all three of us knew his plan was a risk, especially since we didn't have any money to put toward the ransom. Besides covering the checks for the hotel and train, Friedman was in charge of making sure Ruth's mother kept her mouth shut and didn't go to the police or the press. The ink-slinger said he was pretty sure he could convince her to remain quiet and that he even had some kind of tincture which could help calm her.

As we were getting ready to split up, Friedman looked at me and said: "You don't have to do this."

It wasn't like he was volunteering to take my place, and even if he had, I wouldn't have let him because I was afraid the Widow Amy DeFee would hurt, or worse, kill Carrie and Ruth.

"I'm doing it," I said.

"But they might kill you," he blurted.

Like I hadn't already figured that out.

The game against Greeley was difficult. We sold our grandstand and canvas fences to the owner of the Greeley Sugars to pay the crew, who were then let go. I had to pitch, even though it wasn't my turn, and in the written lineup I was listed as Lady Waddell. Folks in Greeley don't know nothing about baseball, so they weren't bothered that I bat and throw right-handed whilst Russ Waddell and Carrie Cassady were left-handers. Well, maybe the fans and players in Greeley thought that Lady Waddell was some switch-pitcher.

We struggled 'cause everybody on our team was uneasy about Carrie and Ruth, the team being without a manager, and the grandstand and fences having been sold and the crew dismissed. But we won, 11-to-7 on account that Greeley fielded a real bad bunch of fat ballists who played like it was a Sunday after a pay day—which it was—and that they had partook of too much John Barleycorn on Saturday night—which they had.

After the game, I put on denim jeans, boots, a bib-front shirt, and a floppy hat of brown wool, sort of what you'd find on baseball players from Boston or Morrisannia way back in the olden times. I didn't think any Greeley folks could identify me as a baseball player, even though I carried my bag.

I watched the Bloomer Girls get on "The C&S Bloomer Girl Special" as well as the two porters, enlisted by Louis Friedman, help get Mrs. Eagan to her berth. I saw Buckskin talking to the conductor before boarding the train, but he didn't even look at me. Wasn't long before the special started hissing and chugging and squeaking and groaning as it left the station, leaving me behind, alone and cold.

With clouds gathering, the wind had picked up and it had turned chilly for August. I wished I'd had a jacket or a coat because I had to start walking south to Fort Vasquez. Jorge at the hotel had told me that Fort Vasquez, if anything was still left of it, lay eighteen miles south.

Maybe a mile out of town, a terrible racket

came up from behind and pulled up beside me. It was an automobile, and nothing like nothing I'd ever seen before. The driver wore a leather helmet, big goggles, linen duster, and scarf.

"Get in," he said once he stopped the thing, then added: "I'm Crazy Uncle Donnie Odom."

The name meant nothing to me, and he wasn't my uncle because my real ma and pa didn't have no siblings. Crazy Uncle Donnie Odom pushed up his goggles, so I could look into his eyes and see that he wasn't lying, I guess.

"Blair Baddeley said to give you a ride to the Fort Vasquez ruins," he told me.

I knew he spoke the truth once he said that, 'cause, excepting me, I don't believe anyone else was aware of this alias Buckskin had used in the past.

After tossing my bag atop what Crazy Uncle Donnie Odom called a rumble seat, I got into the seat next to him. I was nervous, never having been in one of these contraptions before, and when he told me to hold on tight because he didn't go nowhere slow, I became more nervous.

I can tell you, Crazy Uncle Donnie Odom wasn't fooling.

Don't imagine you've ever been in a 1905 Buffum Model G Greyhound Roadster driven by somebody who calls hisself Crazy? I advise you—*Don't do it*—unless, of course, you're bound to save the lives of innocent young ladies.

Once we got out of town, Crazy Uncle Donnie Odom had that automobile going so fast, that all I could do was close my eyes and hold on while bouncing up and down and sideways in the passenger seat. I just prayed that the tires wouldn't fly off or that we wouldn't leap off the road, or that whatever made this thing go wouldn't blow up.

We covered them eighteen miles in no time at all, with Crazy Uncle Donnie Odom yelling to tell me all about the roadster and how it worked. When he stopped the Buffum Greyhound, he almost launched me over the engine and its loud cylinders right into the dirt road. Once my heart resumed beating and Crazy Uncle Donnie Odom quit laughing, he shifted his goggles, reached behind me, grabbed up my bag, handed it to me, and pointed at the side of the road.

"What's left of the trading post is through those cottonwoods, kid. It was an adobe trading post back in the days of the mountain men. Just don't expect to find no Fort McHenry."

Which I hadn't been, having never heard of Fort Vasquez before the previous night or Fort McHenry till Crazy Uncle Donnie Odom brought it up.

After I got out of the roadster on my unsteady legs, Crazy Uncle Donnie Odom lowered his goggles and shifted the gear, and the Buffum roared down the dusty path, leaving me alone, the wind blowing, and something dangersome awaiting me once I got through the cottonwood grove. Didn't know iffen my legs could still recollect how to walk after that nightmare of a ride.

The mountains were behind me, and the cotton-woods gave me some protection from the wind as I moved through them. What lay before me might as well have been Kansas, because it was mostly flat land with a handful of trees scattered across a lot of nothingness. Crazy Uncle Donnie Odom had been right. If there ever had been a fort named Vasquez on these wind-blown plains, the wind had took the adobe away. What was left were a few rounded, misshapen mounds, some scattered rocks, a few piles of rotted trees and wood.

Felt like I'd been walking forever, so I took out the pocket watch that Louis Friedman had given me. Well, he didn't give it to me, as I figured he would want it back. It was a right nice watch, it being a Waltham repeater, solid gold, sixteen jewels, with a name engraved on the back with the date—**May 9, 1888**—with pictures of an older man and woman inside.

I discovered I'd been in among the cottonwoods an hour, so I couldn't wait no longer. I was as scared as I had ever been. Like Buckskin always says, felt like the wings of turkey vultures were flapping around in my belly. Still I made myself step out in the open. The wind practically knocked me down, but I hunched over and moved toward what had once been a trading post. Had to hold the floppy woolen hat on my head with my hand.

When I glanced up, I saw three horses up ahead, saddled but hobbled, and a campfire. The smoke from that fire was being lifted and carried away by the wind about as quickly as it rose above the tall grass and weeds.

I kept moving. When I was almost through the tallest of the weeds, a fellow wearing a long black coat stood up by the fire, and spun around to take notice of me. He hollered something, which caused a dude stretched out on a bedroll to sit up right quick. When he saw me, he threw off his covers, grabbed a gun, and jumped to his feet.

Two men. But three horses. I didn't see Ruth Eagan or Carrie Cassady nowhere.

The two didn't invite me in, but they didn't tell me to stop as I continued to walk toward them. The fire, while not big, looked warm, and after being hauled seventeen miles in a roadster driven by a lunatic and the temperature dropping each and every minute, I wanted to warm my hands. So I went to the fire, laid my bag on the ground, and done what I wanted to do.

"Who are you?" the one in the black coat asked.

"Lucy Totton," I told him.

He give his pard a look, stepped closer, and said: "How did you make it . . . ?" He give a sideways glance at his pard again, who asked: "Was that you in that horseless carriage that we heard out on the road a while back?"

Ignoring the question, I said: "Where are Ruth and Carrie?"

The one who had been sleeping giggled. "Well, they ain't here."

The one in black asked: "Did you bring the money?"

Sighing, I moved back a bit from the fire, and began undoing the knot that held my bag closed. The two licked their lips greedily. From the bag, I withdrew my bat of white ash with red stripes and the big knob at the bottom of the handle that was supposed to offset the weight of the barrel. Holding the bat at my side, I stood and spread my legs out just a little, and gave them a look to let them know that I was serious, even if mighty cold.

The one in the black coat sniggered. Then he pushed back the tail of his coat so I could see the Colt revolver, most likely fully loaded, belted on his hip. The other worked the lever on the repeating rifle, but he didn't aim the Marlin at me.

Instead he said: "Eugene, what kind of fool brings a baseball bat to a gunfight?"

Them were the last words he spoke, or would

speak till them wires got taken out of his jaw, for I swung my bat at him first, on account that he had a cocked rifle in his hands while the pistol remained holstered in the other's gun belt. The rifle holder had pulled the trigger but not before my bat sent blood and teeth flying into the grass and weeds around, which caused the three horses to begin to buck and try to kick loose their hobbles. As the man dropped his rifle and fell, saying garbled words that were impossible to understand, I kept on spinning so that when I had spun all the way around I smacked the bat in the ribs of the black-coated fellow, which sounded awful. I'm guessing more than a few of them got busted. He fell to the ground, dropping his Colt. The look in his eyes said he regretted mightily all his criminal ways because my next swing ended his chance of confessing with spoken words till his jaw mended, too.

That's when the third man, hiding in the prairie like some snake in the grass, fired at me.

CHAPTER TWENTY-THREE

Breckenridge is to have some base ball doings that will enliven things and give the fans something to talk about in the near future. . . . It is supposed the whole populace will turn out to see the fair damsels twirl the sphere, wield the bat and slide for the bases. Old men should wear their glasses.

Breckenridge Bulletin
Breckenridge, Colorado
August 4, 1906

T he momentum and energy used in breaking the jaws of the two ruffians with the baseball bat had made me collapse to the ground, so the bullet from the gun of the third fellow passed over me and spanged off a rock, though it frightened the horses all over again. Scairt me, too, and I moved like a jack rabbit away from the fire and toward what was left of one of Fort Vasquez's walls. I made it just as another bullet knocked dust and pebbles from the broken wall, and I sank low to the ground, clutching my white ash bat as if it could protect me.

I immediately felt like an idiot, for I had crawled right past a Colt revolver and a Marlin rifle, leaving them with the fellows who had planned to shoot me with them. If them two hooligans hadn't been suffering pure agony, they could've used their weapons and I have no doubt I would not be writing this account of what was happening to me.

Then a shot clipped weeds and broke prairie sod near me, and I began to think my chances of leaving what wasn't much of a hiding place and trying to grab the Colt revolver or the Marlin, and then defending myself like the hero in some half-dime novel were slim to none.

The big rifle roared again. The bullet buzzed over my head, and I knew if this kept up, I'd have to make a run for it. There was another shot, but this one sounded like it came from farther out. All was quiet as I tried to plan my next move and listened for movement around me, but all I heard was those two suffering men over by the fire and the spooked horses. The wind started really roaring, and that's all I heard till many minutes later.

"Kid!"

Since the wind was coming from the northwest, I heard my name nice and clear. My heart turned joyful, and I stupidly leaped up and spun around—never thinking that if I was mistaken, the assassin hiding in the prairie grass could shoot me dead.

But I wasn't wrong for Buckskin was headed my way, shoving a man, who staggered as he was pushed right over the little mound I had been hiding behind. Buckskin sent him sprawling into the dirt, and I saw the bloody hole through the assassin's shoulder and knew that this part of Buckskin's plan had worked out none too shabby. I was sure glad he made it.

Being experienced at stock detecting and shooting criminals, Buckskin knew what he was doing. The two villains whose jaws I had busted wouldn't be talking, so my pard swapped his rifle for my bat and stood, spread-legged, over the fellow with the bullet through his shoulder.

"Where are the two girls?" he asked.

"You go to . . . ," the man started to say, but he didn't finish 'cause Buckskin smashed his knee with my bat. The man screamed. To be honest, I almost screamed, too.

"I'll ask you just once more," Buckskin said.

"Breckenridge!" the man shouted, but not all that clearly because he was near crying.

"Where in Breckenridge?" Buckskin asked.

If that man was trying to remember, he took too long. If he was just stalling, he should've knowed better. Buckskin swung the bat again, the man cried out.

"A . . . cave . . . ," he said when he could catch his breathe again. "Or . . . a mine."

"Which one?"

"I . . . I don't know."

Buckskin handed me my bat, and took up his rifle, thumbing back the hammer and aiming the barrel at the man's forehead. "You better answer me straight and quick," Buckskin said. Then he began firing questions, which the man answered without hardly taking more than a second or two to think about each answer.

My Hawthorne bicycle that had carried Buckskin from the railroad tracks two miles out of Greeley all the way here wasn't going to get us back to Greeley before dark. Besides, as cold as it was getting, the three brigands would freeze to death, if they didn't get out of the wind. Buckskin might have been considering riding their horses, but we didn't have to because Crazy Uncle Donnie Odom came roaring up in his Buffum Model G Greyhound Roadster. It was a miracle to me that he had made it all the way out to us. Don't know how he did it.

"Pile in, boys. The Platteville law's on the way," he told us.

We quickly tied up the three injured men and left them where they could be easily found near the fire.

I let Buckskin ride in the front seat, and I got

into the rumble seat so I wouldn't see how close Crazy Uncle Donnie Odom came to killing us all several times, and also so the maniac driver and Buckskin might block some of that numbing wind.

Which turned out to be a good thing 'cause when the roadster took a wild turn once we got back into Greeley, I happened to look up at the train depot. What—or should I say who—I saw made me madder than I'd ever been in my life.

I grabbed Buckskin's shoulder and yelled: "Stop this contraption!"

I had caught a glimpse of Judge Brett as he entered the train, then I caught a glimpse of him through the window as Buckskin and me raced toward the train. He must have passed through the coach I had seen him in, so we hurried into the next car, which wasn't easy as passengers were standing in the aisle as they were getting settled in. The conductor was in this car and he asked to see our tickets, but we just kept moving. Ahead, a fat man in a tweed coat and a woman in the shiny orange dress were calling out to the conductor as they were shoved aside by Brett as he moved through the car. Whilst they was complaining about the nerve of some folks, me and Buckskin hustled to the smoking car and I pointed out Judge Kevin Brett to Buckskin.

At the same time, Brett looked back, and,

seeing us, he yelled out for help. At this, two men rose out of their seats.

Buckskin and me didn't stop walking till we stood in front of the three men, two of whom I thought might've been the Kelton brothers, but they weren't.

Believing he was protected, the judge grew in confidence, saying: "Boys, this is Buck Skinner. And the boy is a runaway. Wanted by his mother in Breckenridge."

The two men smiled at each other and turned to face Judge Brett.

"We aren't interested in them," said the taller of the two. "It's you and your friend, Amy DeFee, we're after. We're with the Pinkertons and we've . . ."

I didn't really hear the rest of what he said as relief washed through and over me.

As for Brett, he fell to his knees, crying out for mercy and forgiveness. He blamed the widow for his crimes, promising he'd tell them everything she had done if they would be lenient with him.

I smiled at Buckskin as we followed the two Pinkertons who led Judge Kevin Brett off the train.

Buckskin tells me that I need to slow this next part down, so it don't read like a cattle stampede but more like a baseball game, which he often likens to a chess match, which I ain't never played, poker being the game of choice on train rides, while, during ball games, the guys preferred tobacco juice spitting, which my girl teammates and I found disgusting. I understand what Buckskin means, though, as some folks think that baseball ain't much different than watching wheat grow, because they don't understand the nuances—a word Buckskin just taught me—of the sport, and besides, sometimes baseball can seem like a cattle stampede, like what I witnessed in Breckenridge, Colorado, which I'll tell you about directly. Well, you'd best take a deep breath and let it out slowly, before I commence to tell what all happened after Judge Brett got carted to jail.

At the Greeley Police Station, Police Chief Perry Stokes listened to Buckskin and me, then telephoned the sheriff down in Platteville and listened to him, too, but I don't reckon Chief Stokes cared much about nothing he'd just heard until the Pinkerton detectives told him what they knew.

Those detectives, who prefer to be called *operatives* and who asked not to be identified by name in my narrative, *The Sporting News*, or *Variety*, explained all they had learned about the Widow Amy DeFee's long history of crimes throughout the Midwest. Turns out, the agency had been investigating that contemptible woman for better than fifteen months, but didn't get enough evidence until the widow had hired these two Pinkertons, who were posing as cheap gunmen. The agency had been put on the widow's trail after a longtime employee of the Romeo & Juliet Marriage Plan Company in Kansas City, Missouri, had suspicioned the widow's entry for the 1907 yearbook—yes, the Widow Amy DeFee planned to continue her horrible sins—because it reminded him of an entry he recollected from the annual catalog of 1897, and because another operative recalled receiving a letter from an ice-plant worker in Medicine Lodge, Kansas, who thought something stank about how a friend had choked to death on an apple two months after he married a widow in 1895 whose information had been clipped out of a copy of the Romeo & Juliet Marriage Plan Company's catalog from the previous year. And every single time, even in the forthcoming publication for next year, that vile, vain woman claimed to be twenty-nine years old. As I write this, by the way, the Romeo & Juliet Marriage Plan Company is deader than the Leadville Blues, but I sure hope that longtime worker who contacted the Pinkerton National Detective Agency soon finds gainful employment at a reputable mail-order-bride service.

While the two Pinkerton operatives showed Chief Stokes lots of notes and what they called affidavits, plus sketches and even fingerprints, Buckskin told the operatives: "You Pinkertons are to law enforcement what the Cincinnati Red Stockings of 'Sixty-Nine are to baseball." Though I nodded, deep down I could not help but wonder that had those detectives acted quicker, Pa might still be alive. Nothing could bring Pa back, so I reminded Buckskin, Pinkertons, and Greeley's peace officers: "Ruth and Carrie remain in grave danger."

That's when Crazy Uncle Donnie Odom and some sheriff's deputies brung in the hired gunmen who'd been captured at the Fort Vasquez ruins, and while two couldn't talk so good, they all pointed to the judge when asked if the man who had hired them "to commit this most heinous felony" was in the police station. All three ruffians got hauled down to the jail cells, though a deputy promised to send for a doctor, but that mustn't have happened till after I left.

Once the door closed, Chief Stokes slapped Judge Brett twice, which the Pinkertons pretended not to see. "You got ten seconds," the chief said, "to start talking or choke on an apple." Judge Brett argued that he deserved—but I don't know what he thought he deserved because the next slap shut the judge up for a little bit. "This is the West, by thunder," Chief Stokes said, "and you're down to five seconds." For the next four minutes, Judge Brett told us all about the widow and her plans, and, most importantly, the location of the old mine near Breckenridge where Ruth and Carrie were being held hostage.

As the sobbing judge got drug to the stairs that led to the cells, one of the Pinkerton men used the telephone to call another operative in Greeley to ask him to telegraph the law in Breckenridge. The curse told Buckskin and me that something was wrong.

The Pinkerton operative said, "Wire's dead."

Chief Stokes said: "Storm, most likely."

Buckskin said: "How can we get to Breckenridge?"

Crazy Uncle Donnie Odom said: "My sister's engineer on a freight train that ought to be leaving in a jiffy."

The other Pinkerton operative said: "Your sister?"

Crazy Uncle Donnie Odom said: "Don't tell nobody."

"Keep trying to telegraph the Breckenridge law," Buckskin ordered, and I followed him, with Crazy Uncle Donnie Odom and one of the Pinkerton operatives right behind us. Buckskin and me carried our baseball bags. Louis Friedman never quite figured why we'd carry baseball equipment to rescue two kidnapped girls, but he's just a correspondent, not a professional athlete.

Upon hearing our story, Crazy Uncle Donnie Odom's sister, who didn't look at all like a woman, spit tobacco juice into the wind, and told the Pinkerton operative to uncouple everything except the tinder, and pulled me into the cab. Buckskin climbed in without assistance, while Crazy Uncle Donnie Odom helped the Pinkerton operative uncouple the freight cars. Another railroad man, holding a lantern, ran up to the edge of the tracks.

"Phil," he demanded, "what the Sam Hill's going on?"

"Roscoe," Crazy Uncle Donnie Odom's sister told the fireman, "charge."

The Baldwin pulled out of the yard, leaving boxcars behind—not to mention Crazy Uncle Donnie Odom, the Pinkerton operative, and the conductor (or whatever he was). The Pinkerton operative slipped on the slick ground, causing Crazy Uncle Donnie Odom and the angry railroad official to trip over him, else the Baldwin's cab would've been really cramped all the way to Breckenridge. Yet as we picked up speed, another figure suddenly ran alongside the rails, his yells drowned out by the noise from the locomotive. After tossing his bag, the one holding bats and a Winchester, onto the metal floor, Buckskin leaned out. Likewise, I dropped my bat bag and grabbed hold of Buckskin's waistband with my left hand while clinging as hard as I could to something cold and metal with my right. Laughing, Crazy Uncle Donnie Odom's sister pushed the throttle, not caring one whit if the fellow running, Buckskin, and me all tumbled out to die gruesome deaths, which, coming from a railroad town, I'd seen more than I'd care to remember.

Luckily, Buckskin pulled the man into the cab, and we all fell into a heap. I sat up, shook my aching head, and cussed the Pinkerton operative—but it wasn't a Pinkerton man after all. It wasn't Crazy Uncle Donnie Odom, either.

It was Louis Friedman, who looked like he'd been rolling around in prairie grass and mud for days.

Buckskin turned savage. "What are you doing here? You're supposed to be in Breckenridge with the girls."

"I'm following the story." Friedman's dander was up, too. "And Ruth. And my best chances of finding both are by sticking with you two." He jabbed a scraped finger at Buckskin and me.

"Charge." The engineer tooted the whistle long and loud. "Charge, boys, charge."

Charge is exactly what we did, into the night, into worsening weather.

As we rode the rails, I got to thinking about all the work it took to get to Breckenridge.

"It takes a special train to stop at Breckenridge?" I yelled over the roar and wind at Buckskin.

"On this line," he answered.

"Well then, how did the Widow Amy DeFee get Ruth and Carrie there so quick?" A contemptible woman like the Widow Amy DeFee would not splurge on a special train, secrecy being one of the keys to successful kidnapping and blackmailing.

Before Buckskin could answer, the engineer chuckled. "She could take another outfit. The Denver, South Park, and Pacific started hauling folks back in 'Eighty-Two. Or take a Colorado and Southern people-carrier to Denver, then ride another line to Silverthorne or Dillon. Easy enough to rent a wagon, hack, or horses, or take the stage to Breckenridge. Cheaper, too." He—I mean, *she*—spit tobacco juice out the window. "Or foot it by the ankle express, though that can be risky any time of the year."

I studied on that for a moment, before asking Buckskin: "Well, if that's cheaper, how come you got a special train for the Bloomer Girls?"

My brain must've still been addled, my question having nothing to do with the jeopardy Ruth and Carrie remained in at that moment.

Buckskin gave me a look that said I was a dolt. "Because we're baseball players," he snapped.

If you haven't been to Breckenridge, I should tell you that it is way high in the Rockies, better than nine thousand feet—double the altitude of Greeley.

As our special train climbed toward the mining town where Ruth, Carrie, and the Widow Amy DeFee waited, the world turned stark white.

"We can't get through this, Phil," the fireman hollered. "Not without a snowplow."

But Phil—short, I'm guessing, for Phyllis—Odom quoted Admiral Farragut from the battle of Mobile Bay in 1864, shouting: "Damn the torpedoes, full speed ahead!" At least that's the way Louis Friedman recalled it in *The Sporting News*.

Snow came down even harder when the train stopped at Breckenridge. Two men wearing badges greeted us.

"Which one of you plays for the Bloomers?" one asked.

"I do," Buckskin and I shouted at the same time.

The lawman blinked. Crazy Aunt Phyllis Odom chuckled.

Louis Friedman, Buckskin, and I leaped out of the cab, where the firebox had kept us warm, into bitterly cold air.

"Have you found the hostages?" Friedman asked.

"Yes," the first lawman answered. "The telegraph from Greeley was received roughly two hours ago."

"Neither girl was harmed," the second lawman said. "The kidnapper surrendered without resistance."

Relief swept over me. "Praise God, you've captured the Widow Amy DeFee."

"Widow?" the first lawman said. "No, it was Round Tree Russell holding the ladies. A local ruffian. We're beating a better confession out of him now."

My heart broke like a cheap bat.

"We have a hack," the second lawman said.

Thus, the two deputies, me, Buckskin, Friedman, and Crazy Aunt Phyllis Odom—who said he sure wanted to see this, thinking we were going to watch the game—piled into the hack. The hack, by the way, was a buckboard, with no cover, so we got snowed on all the way to the courthouse, where we learnt that Ruth and Carrie had been found in the abandoned mine, just where Judge Brett had said they would be. The villain watching the two had surrendered without any shooting, and had been taken into custody. The girls insisted that they would play against Breckenridge. Two policemen had escorted the ballists to the park.

"They're playing baseball?" Louis Friedman said. "After all they've been through?"

"They're playing baseball?" Buckskin asked. "In this weather?"

Only I kept my senses intact after the harrowing

ride and freezing temperatures. "Where's the Widow Amy DeFee?"

"Federal, local, and county lawmen are searching for her," the county sheriff said. "The judge will be here directly. And the Pinkertons are sending a special train from Denver after the storm passes." The Pinkertons must have figured they was as good as baseball players and deserved special trains, too.

In protest, I stamped my cold feet on the floor, thinking that *after the storm passes* could be days.

"The widow will be at the ball park," Buckskin announced.

The sheriff, who had little experience in the wickedness of the Widow Amy DeFee, said: "In this weather?"

We left him in his toasty office. The hack had vanished. But Buckskin, knowing the location of the baseball park since he had arranged this game, ran through the cold, white wall. Louis Friedman, Crazy Aunt Phyllis Odom, and two deputies followed. I ran alongside Buckskin. I would've been ahead of him, but I didn't know where the park was, and couldn't see nothing but snow.

A deputy's badge got us into the park without paying two bits each, and we huddled together. We couldn't let the Widow Amy DeFee recognize us or get suspicious, Buckskin told us, and

261

explained how we would enter the stands by different entrances, find a place to sit, watch, and be inconspicuous. Buckskin relieved a shivering peanut salesman of his wares, pulled on the peanut vender's cap, too, but gave one of the deputies the bag that secreted his Winchester. After wishing us all luck, he moved toward the third-base-line entrance. I kept my bag, though it didn't hold no firearm, and when it was my turn to venture into the grandstands, I swapped hats with the ticket-seller, and went up the same way Buckskin had gone.

The grandstands weren't packed, not in this weather, but the game was still being played. Along the first-base entrance, I saw Friedman find a seat on the first row. One deputy huddled in the shadows near home plate. Didn't see Crazy Aunt Phyllis Odom.

When the other deputy appeared on the first-base side, Louis Friedman moved toward us, as nonchalantly as a body could do on such a miserable afternoon. He stopped to ask the man huddled underneath a snow-covered bear-skin next to us if he knew the score. That's a sports reporter for you, interested in the contest, not justice.

The man answered in a frosty breath: "Breckenridge . . . four to one, bottom of the seventh inning. Bloomers won the toss and elected to be home."

"Peanuts!" Buckskin called out. "Peanuts!" He moved away from us, being, I reckon, inconspicuous. No one appeared hungry. When Buckskin walked back toward us, he said to me: "Where the heck is Amy DeFee?" I'll let you decide if he said *heck* or something else. Both of us knew that that evil woman, expecting a $5,000 payoff to be delivered by Buckskin, had to be at the baseball park since she had no idea that her plan had blown up.

At that moment, I cared not about the Widow Amy DeFee's whereabouts or the score of the game. "Where are Ruth and Carrie?" I asked.

All of us turned toward the Bloomer Girls' bench. The players were huddled together. I couldn't make out a single face.

Friedman turned to the man under the bear-skin. "Have two Bloomer Girls recently joined their teammates?"

"In this weather?" The man snorted.

"They should be here by now," Friedman moaned.

My heart sank. Could the Widow Amy DeFee have foully murdered the lawmen escorting Ruth and Carrie and taken my precious teammates hostage again?

"Might've got lost in this whiteout," the fellow underneath the bear-skin suggested.

"Spread out," Buckskin ordered us, ignoring the man sheltered under the bear-skin.

Batting my eyes against the snow, I tried to make out the faces around the field, or find two girls running toward the Bloomers' bench. Finally I spied, not my teammates, but the wickedest witch of the West, for where else would that hag be but on the bench with the Breckenridge Nine? My whole body tensed. In spite of the cold, fire consumed me. So, pulling my baseball bat out of my bag—yes, it still remained with me, professional ballist that I had become—I made a beeline toward our rival's bench.

The wind carried Buckskin's cry: "Kid, no!" For he must have seen the murdering fiend, too. Like when a coach signaled me to stop at third base when I knew I could score, I paid Buckskin no mind. Down the stands, leaping onto the ground, moving through the gate near the Breckenridge bench. No one stopped me. Most of the spectators and park officials, I figured, were too cold to care.

Wearing one of the Breckenridge Nine's Chicago pillbox ball caps, yellow, though they called it gold, with two rows of black wool stripes and a black visor, the Widow Amy DeFee appeared to be focusing on the deputy staying out of sight—out of the wind, he later conceded—by home plate. Not me. Not Buckskin. Not Friedman. Suddenly, her head jerked toward the first-base bench, and she jumped to her feet, cursing vilely, loud enough for me to hear.

I twisted my head to see what had agitated her. The sight of Ruth and Carrie running toward the Bloomer Girls' bench lifted my spirits. Yes, we learned and Friedman reported later, they had gotten lost on the way from the courthouse to the park. Their escorts blamed the weather, but I credit that chief umpire in the sky.

The arrival of Ruth and Carrie cheered the Kansas City National Bloomer Girls, too. They might have been losing, the snow might have started blowing sideways, but this team was intact once more, though without Buckskin and me. And there was still plenty of baseball to be played, providing the umpire did not call the game because of the weather.

Realizing the two kidnapped girls had been freed, the Widow Amy DeFee whirled, perhaps searching for Judge Brett, who was locked up inside the Greeley jail, although she didn't know that. Then, just as the snow slackened and the wind died down—perhaps another gift from the Almighty—that nefarious woman spotted me.

Consumed with rage, she screamed, knocked a Breckenridge player into the slush, and ran— where I blocked her nearest exit. Instead of setting my feet and playing my position, I dashed to meet her challenge, like I was coming in to bare-hand a slow roller. Only . . . my feet and legs flew out in front of me, I landed hard, and slid across icy sod toward the widow on my hindquarters, spinning like an out-of-control sleigh, yet still clutching my white-ash, red-stripe bat. It's not the way I wanted to meet my nemesis, and, thankfully, it wasn't mentioned in *The Sporting News*. But luck stayed with me. My bat caught my evil stepmother just below her knees, knocking her to the ground, hard, leaving her writhing in pain. I would have kept right on sliding across the diamond toward the Bloomer Girls' dugout if Katie Maloney, leading off third base in foul territory with two outs, hadn't run over to stop me.

"Hey!" Katie looked down at me. "What's going on?"

Breckenridge's catcher shouted—"Grove!"— and rifled the ball he had just taken from the pitcher at the third baseman, Grove, hoping to catch Katie in a rundown and get her out. But Grove, staring at me, the widow, and Katie Maloney, never even glimpsed the ball as it sailed past and disappeared in the snow in left field. Louis Friedman reported in *The Sporting News* that with two strikes and two outs, the catcher shouldn't have worried about a meaningless run on third base.

Seeing it all, Maggie Casey bellowed at Katie to run. She did and she scored, cutting Breckenridge's lead to two.

As for me, I planned to stove in Amy DeFee's

skull with my baseball bat, but first I needed the bat to push me back to my feet.

The black-hearted widow, though crying in pain, managed to sit up. Her brow shriveled into a deep creases as Breckenridge constables, including Carrie and Ruth's escorts and a few others, blew their whistles while swarming onto the snow-covered field. A Breckenridge player, perhaps wanted for crimes of his own, ran for the nearest exit. The foul-murdering woman tried to stand, only to slip again on the ice. The Breckenridge hurler whistled at Katie Maloney, who, bending over before the Bloomer Girls bench, kept brushing the ice off her bloomers and stockings.

With snowflakes driving into my eyes, but bat in my hands, I moved toward the woman who helped kill my pa. The bat rose over my head, but I couldn't see the widow well enough to bust her jaw—not because of the snow, but because of my tears. Or maybe, just maybe, I ain't some heartless, murdering scoundrel. Buckskin's pleading voice also squashed my thirst for vengeance.

"Let the law handle her, kid. Don't do anything you'll regret. Don't do anything that your mother . . . your real mother and father . . . wouldn't want you to do."

The bat slipped out of my hands, dropped to the snow, as constabularies grabbed the widow and slapped manacles on her. They had quite a time hauling her off to jail, what with her bucking, hissing, spitting, and cussing like some hydrophoby she-wolf.

Buckskin asked the lawmen if it would be all right for us to watch the rest of the ball game. He promised that we'd return to the courthouse afterward. With the widow raising such a ruction, the peace officers didn't protest too much, and two sheriff's deputies said they wanted to watch the game, too, but I warrant they just didn't want to get scratched up and spit on by the woman they were arresting. So the widow got dragged out of the snow by officers whose patience quickly vanished, and Buckskin, me, and our associates and escorts climbed up into the stands to watch the rest of the game. Buckskin and I took refuge underneath the old-timer's bear-skin, where we sat shivering until the bottom of the ninth inning.

During which something happened I had never seen happen in no baseball game before. And probably never will again.

With the Bloomer Girls staring at defeat, I wondered if the Widow Amy DeFee would be allowed to collect the winnings from her bet, but quickly dismissed the idea from my mind, because I didn't really care.

Maggie Casey led off the last of the ninth inning. She smacked a ball that surely would've flown out of the park on any normal day, but wind and snow forced it into the glove of Breckenridge's right fielder.

One out.

Next up, Pearl Murphy singled sharply, and stole second base on the first pitch to Maud Nelson, but then Maud grounded out to the first baseman, although that sent Pearl to third base.

Two outs.

The snow started coming down harder again.

Carrie Cassady hit for Gypsie O'Hearn, who was suffering near frostbite in her fingers from her valiant effort at pitching. But Carrie, having been held hostage in cave, wasn't at her best.

Strike one.

That ball was a mile outside, but Carrie, nervous, swung and missed, but the ball went past the catcher, too, and over to the fence where it bounced off and headed toward the Breckenridge bench. The catcher slipped while chasing after it, which let Pearl Murphy make it home to score. We were down by one run.

Strike two.

It was hard for Carrie to see with the snow blowing in her face.

Strike three.

Suddenly exhausted from everything that had happened since we'd first arrived in Greeley, I slumped and groaned. We had lost to Breckenridge. The game was over. Buckskin, though, leaped from underneath the bear-skin and started yelling.

"Run! Run! Run, Carrie, run!"

Maggie Casey hollered the same thing.

The umpire stepped aside, the catcher stood up, and the Breckenridge team captain thundered: "Get the ball! Get the ball! Throw her out!"

You see, the ball had sailed right over the catcher's head, not that you could blame him, for the snow kept hammering his face, too, but there's a rule that not everybody knows and that's this: The batter ain't out on the third strike unless the catcher catches the pitch cleanly. If he doesn't, the batter can run, and if he reaches first base before the catcher can tag him out or throw the ball to first and have the first baseman step on the bag or tag the batter before he gets there, well, the runner is safe at first. However, that rule doesn't apply if there's a runner already on first base (which, in this case, there wasn't), unless, of course, there are two outs (which, in this case, there was). Yes, the rule has been tinkered with over the years, but that was the rule, is the rule, and Carrie Cassady ran all the way to first base before the catcher found the ball and threw it, but he threw it way too hard and too high. Carrie Cassady made it to second base by the time the ball came back to the pitcher, and he wasn't happy.

Tying run on second. But still two outs. Jessie Dailey's turn to bat.

There's a reason Mr. Norris, that scoundrel, had Jessie Dailey selling tickets or programs more often than she played on the field. Her hitting wasn't so good.

Strike one.

Ball one.

Ball two.

Strike two.

I closed my eyes, and not because of the snow. Then I heard the crack of the bat.

My eyes opened to see both the second baseman and the shortstop lunging over second base. I watched the snow spray all around as the ball rolled toward center field, and then I turned into one of those banshees. Buckskin cheered. Even the man with the bear-skin jumped up and down, though he hailed from Breckenridge so you'd have thought he'd be pulling for the home team and wanting this game to end so he could go home to a warm fireplace and hot toddy.

Carrie scored easily, and when the center fielder threw the ball to the plate, which he shouldn't have done, Jessie Dailey had enough savvy to run to second. She slid in well ahead of the tag and was safe.

Two outs. Score tied. Winning run on second base.

Ruth grabbed a bat from the bench and stepped toward the plate.

Sucking in a breath that froze my lungs, I

whispered—"That's my bat,"—'cause it was, I recognized it. And though I had intended to bash in the widow's brains with it, I must've dropped it and, somehow, it ended up over by the Bloomer Girls' bench, where Ruth had picked it up.

My bat was way too big for a little girl like Ruth Eagan.

Strike one.

Ball one.

Good, I told myself, *she was smart enough to lay off that pitch.* I held my breath as the pitcher started his windup. Snowflakes swirled. I sucked in a deep breath. The wind blew. The pitch was delivered.

Ruth swung. We all heard the crack. We saw the pitcher slip on the snow as the ball bounced through his legs, saw Jessie Dailey running toward third, rounding it, as the ball again went right up the middle into center field. Then every Bloomer Girl charged off the bench, and the Breckenridge boys, those on the field and those standing in front of their bench, dropped to their knees, and the six Breckenridge fans—not the man who shared his bear-skin with me and Buckskin—stood, their mouths open in disbelief. The Bloomer Girls had come from behind to win a game they would have lost if not for that glorious dropped third strike.

Later, I thought about how much I wanted to

be there when Amy DeFee learnt that she'd not only lost her freedom, but her bet. But for that glorious moment, me and Buckskin and the man with the bear-skin were jumping up and down, slapping each other on the back, crying with joy. Louis Friedman ran onto the field. And Crazy Aunt Phyllis Odom, who I'd done lost track of, hollered from the top of the grandstands: "Girls rule! Men stink! Girls rule! Men stink!"

After the best game I had ever seen was over, Crazy Aunt Phyllis Odom went to the depot to fetch his Baldwin and find his fireman and return to Greeley to get the rest of his train, while the deputy led Buckskin, Friedman, and me to the courthouse. It was a good thing we went because the Breckenridge judge was named DeFee, too—Larry DeFee—and the widow kept batting her eyes at him and trying to look pitiful. Somehow she had even managed to talk them into taking the manacles off her wrists.

As we stood in the back of the room stomping the snow off from our shoes and clothes, the widow spotted us, and, pointing at us, she yelled at the Breckenridge jurist: "Larry, these are the scoundrels and killers!"

She directed anger and accusations mostly at Buckskin, saying he was a murdering friend of the killer Tom Horn and that there was a reward posted on him in Wyoming, and that if anybody needed to get his neck stretched, it was Buckskin Compton.

But Buckskin weren't no killer.

Smiling, he pulled something out of his pocket as he walked to Judge DeFee. "Here," he said, and let this newspaper article get passed around to those in charge. It had run in a June edition of the *Globe-Republican* out of Dodge City, which, it turns out, was another reason Buckskin volunteered to come to Colorado to arrange these baseball games. It was just a one paragraph, short, didn't even get a headline, just listed as one of the **News From The Wires**, and it read:

More shenanigans in northeastern Wyoming, where an angry mob took the Kelton brothers out of jail and hoisted them to Hades with hemp. The brothers had been arrested for killing Judge T.T. Shoumacher, their uncle, who they said owed them $500 for months spent chasing the "murderer" of two of the judge's sons, even though a grand jury refused to return a true bill of indictment because of the nature of the judge's no-account sons, Wilbur and Thad, who will be missed in the Powder River country about as much as Judge Shoumacher, or his other son, now serving a twenty-five-year sentence in Rawlings, or the Kelton boys.

So, Buckskin had proven to Judge DeFee, various lawmen, and the Widow Amy DeFee that he wasn't wanted nowhere for nothing.

After that was taken care of, Judge Larry DeFee asked me to tell all I knew. I felt like maybe this was finally justice as I explained how the two had killed my father, had tried to kill me, how they had blackmailed me and Buckskin, and kidnapped Ruth and Carrie, among other crimes.

By the time I was finished, Amy DeFee knew she couldn't be looking to Judge Larry DeFee for help anymore, because he turned to her and said: "If this is all true . . . and I believe it is . . . you are a vile, repulsive, mean, contemptible person who tarnishes the name DeFee and all honest athletes across the West. Take off that baseball cap, you poor excuse for a woman. You're not fit to wear that crown of honor."

Buckskin and me smiled at each other as they led the widow off to a jail cell. Yet, somehow, I hoped they wouldn't beat a confession out of her. Don't ask me why. I wasn't forgiving her or nothing like that. Beating up prisoners just didn't seem right—like an umpire widening the strike zone because the batsman was a scoundrel—even when they deserved it.

Thus ends my mostly honest account of how I avenged my pa's foul murder in Pleasanton, Kansas, way over in Colorado just before a blizzard left a ton of snow covering a right pretty baseball field—in early August, mind you.

EPILOGUE

The Bloomers sure play ball and no foolishness about it. They are not the handsomest women that ever ate Boston baked beans, but are stout healthy, agreeable and astute girls, who take a good natured roast, and give back as good as is sent. Our boys were fairly beaten.

Cherokee County Republican
Baxter Springs, Kansas
September 13, 1906

Riding this train west, Buckskin says I need to tie up all them loose ends, before I send this here narrative to the editor of the All-Sports Library. Louis Friedman, who ain't the louse I figured him for, says I have a crackerjack tale. More importantly, since Friedman knows the editor who publishes them five-penny dreadfuls, he said he will put in a word for me as he's certain his friend will publish this here book and I'll make a fortune.

We shall see.

Regarding those loose ends Buckskin mentioned, Governor Hoch and Attorney General

277

Jackson got the Widow Amy DeFee and Judge Kevin Brett extradited from the Colorado jails back to Pleasanton, Kansas. The rest of her gang got tarred and feathered, except them whose jaws got busted because the good folks of Colorado figured those boys had suffered enough.

The Kansas trial didn't last but two days as Judge Wheeler "maintained a stern countenance"—so noted *The Pleasanton Herald*—and didn't tolerate no nonsense in his court. He sentenced Judge Kevin Brett to twenty-five years at hard labor after that cur turned what's called state's evidence, meaning that he told the truth, whole truth, and nothing but the truth—mostly—about all that he had done at the Widow Amy DeFee's behest. Three Pinkerton detectives testified, too, telling how they'd been hired to investigate the widow's background. They found a string of crimes under various names she had committed before she even landed in Kansas. The widow testified, too, but it didn't do no good because Judge Wheeler instructed the jury that they should not let the witness's "crocodile tears" influence their verdict. He also upheld a lot of the state solicitor's objections, and told the jury to ignore the widow's lawyer stuttering, which he felt the attorney was using to confuse the jury and gain sympathy for the widow.

The jury found the Widow Amy DeFee guilty of every indictment, numbering sixteen, and while Judge Larry DeFee of Breckenridge had requested the widow be extradited back to the State of Colorado after the Kansas trial so she could be tried for kidnapping and graft and a slew of other charges, Judge Wheeler said there wouldn't be no need for that since he was sentencing the Widow Amy DeFee to be hanged—actually, he said hung, but nobody, not even Buckskin, corrected him—by the neck until she was dead, dead, dead.

That's when the Widow Amy DeFee got ashen-faced, and swooned, and her lawyer cried out: "J-j-j-judge, you ca-ca-ca-cannot hang a-a-a l-l-lady."

The judge hammered his gavel a few times and said: "Counselor, I'm not hanging a *lady*."

Buckskin reckons they'll likely commute the sentence to life, but that life in Lansing ain't no life at all.

Buckskin and me rode the Frisco down to Baxter Springs for the Bloomer Girls baseball game. We weren't decked out like girls and we even had to pay two bits each to get into the new grandstand that the re-hired old crew had put up 'cause the new Bloomer Girl taking tickets didn't know who we were.

Maggie Casey coached the girls and still played right field, at least up until she got thrown out of the game by the umpire. Ruth Eagan did a fine job at first base, and started the rally in the last inning, just after Maggie Casey got tossed by the deputy sheriff who was umpiring. Louis Friedman was there taking notes for some article he'd be writing for *The Sporting News* or *Variety* or whoever might pay him, even though he didn't need no money 'cause his family owned about half of Topeka. We sure owe his family a pile of gratitude. Especially, for the money from his family that allowed Friedman to take over the National Bloomer Girls of Kansas City and buy a new portable grandstand and canvas fences. Mr. Norris ain't been seen or heard from since he never showed up in Greeley. He's suspected of disappearing into Mexico. I hope he eats some bad oysters.

After that ball game, the Bloomer Girls and the Baxter Springs boys shook hands and they were all in high spirits. As I stood there watching, Buckskin asked me if I wanted to go down and say hello or good bye to the girls.

But I didn't want to. "I've said my good byes," I told him, and watched Louis Friedman and Ruth Eagan hold hands as they left the field together while the crew took down the equipment.

Buckskin and me took another train to Kansas City, where I reckon this story sort of started back in 1897 when I first taken notice of baseball as a seven-year-old. There, Buckskin told me we were heading out again, though I wasn't sure where we were going.

As the train rumbled along, Buckskin said: "I think Maggie will do a good job."

"She kicked dirt all over home plate," I reminded him.

He nodded.

"Over the umpire's shoes," I added.

Another nod.

"Then after the umpire warned her, she went back to the bench, grabbed a bucket of baseballs, and dumped them all over home plate."

"Yeah," Buckskin said. "That'll be some story in *The Sporting News*."

"What Maggie done wasn't nice."

"Kid, baseball isn't always about being nice. Maggie wasn't doing that because she thought the umpire was an idiot. She did it to throw some fire into the bellies of the Bloomer Girls. And it worked. Four consecutive singles followed. Baxter Springs fell apart. The pitcher lost control. The Bloomer Girls couldn't lose after that, and Baxter Springs had no chance of winning. All of that was Maggie's doing. She'll be some manager and coach. I'll have to remember that when we get to Salida."

"Salida?" I asked.

Grinning, he reached into his coat pocket and showed me one of them yellow telegraph papers. Salida, I read, had offered Buckskin the job of managing their team, and since we were on a westbound train, I figured he'd taken the job. And iffen that telegrapher didn't make no mistake, I don't blame him for accepting. The amount they were willing to pay him seemed mighty fine.

"Ain't Salida where they lynched the fellow who had been coaching their team?" I asked.

"Yeah."

"Don't that make you nervous?"

He chuckled. "He wasn't hung for losing ball games. And I don't plan on robbing any store."

"Hanged," I told him. "Not hung."

"Nice job, kid. I was testing you."

The train clicked along the rails. I felt myself getting sleepy.

"By the way," he said, "I need a second baseman."

At those words, I felt wide awake.

"Ain't Salida where them geese was in the outfield?" I asked.

"Yeah."

"That was a pretty town," I recollected.

He told me what Salida paid its ballists, which weren't as much as I'd gotten with the Bloomer Girls but considerable more than the Widow Amy DeFee had ever allowed me to keep. I leaned back and pictured that waitress in Salida who'd talked to me about geese and trout and had come to the ball game and cheered us on the same that she did the Salida players. She sure was sweet and pretty, meaning the waitress in Salida, and not Ruth. I even began hoping that Louis Friedman would make Ruth happy.

"You got yourself a second baseman," I told Buckskin.

Buckskin held out his hand, and we shook.

Then he said: "There's just one more thing, kid. Get your hair cut. I won't have any player on my club who looks like a girl."

AUTHOR'S NOTE

An Emporia boy, whose name is withheld because it is his first offence and also on account of his parents, is playing baseball in another state with the Boston Bloomer girls!

The Emporia Gazette
Emporia, Kansas
August 20, 1906

The epigraphs, like the one above, along with most of the names of the Bloomer Girls, are about all that's true in this novel.

History records that most Bloomer baseball teams had a few male players disguised as women when they played town teams not just across the American West, but the entire United States. Kansas City fielded just one of many "National" Bloomer teams.

The idea for this novel came about while reading Gerald C. Wood's *Smoky Joe Wood: The Biography of a Baseball Legend* (University of Nebraska Press, 2013) and from watching Billy Wilder's 1959 movie comedy *Some Like It Hot* too often. Wood was a young teen when he played for the Kansas City Bloomer Girls in 1906. Other sources include *Women in Baseball: The Forgotten History* by Gai Ingham Berlage (Praeger, 1994) and *Bloomer Girls: Women Baseball Pioneers* by Debra A. Shattuck (University of Illinois Press, 2017).

The Bloomer Girls' final comeback in Breckenridge is a not-quite-literal though fairly faithful recreation (except for the setting and the snow) of my favorite Little League baseball victory as a coach. My wife says she had never seen me look so happy when I ran and hugged the boy who scored the walk-off, winning run. If you could've seen the smile on the boy's face, you'd understand why.

I should also thank the Colorado State Library; Denver Public Library; Kansas State Historical Society; Missouri State Historical Society; University of Maryland Archives; the Giamatti Research Center at the National Baseball Hall of Fame and Museum in Cooperstown, New York; and Newspapers.com and NewspaperArchive. com.

For any reader who paid really close attention, I tip my Kansas City Royals cap to Jack Schaefer and Charles Portis, master writers who helped point me on this career path, and sprinkled in a few other names of Western writers. And a deep thanks to all the Little League parents who trusted me with their ballplayers as a board officer, coach, and umpire. Finally, heartfelt appreciation to my literary agents, Vicki Piekarski and the late Jon Tuska, for putting up with me for twenty years, for their eagle eyes and wise counsel, and for letting me write—for the most part—what I wanted to write.

Johnny D. Boggs
Santa Fe, New Mexico

ABOUT THE AUTHOR

In 2019, Johnny D. Boggs won his eighth Spur Award from Western Writers of America— the most in the nonprofit association's 66-year history. *Booklist* has called him "among the best Western writers at work today," and *Publishers Weekly* said: "Boggs's narrative voice captures the old-fashioned style of the past."

A native of South Carolina and former newspaper journalist in Texas, Boggs has written historical Westerns (*Greasy Grass*; *Hard Way Out of Hell*); traditional novels (*The Big Fifty*; *MacKinnon*); comic novels (*East of the Border*; *Mojave*); baseball Westerns (*Camp Ford*; *The Kansas City Cowboys*); Civil War novels (*Wreaths of Glory*; *And There I'll Be a Soldier*); Colonial/Revolutionary War novels (*The Cane Creek Regulators*; *Ghost Legion*); Western mysteries (the Killstraight series); young-adult fiction (*Doubtful Cañon*; *South by Southwest*; *Taos Lightning*); and nonfiction (*Jesse James and the Movies*; *Billy the Kid on Film, 1911-2012*; *The American West on Film*); along with short fiction and short nonfiction. His Spur Awards came for his short story "A Piano at Dead Man's Crossing" (2002) and for his novels *Camp Ford* (2006), *Doubtful Cañon* (2008), *Hard Winter*

(2010), *Legacy of a Lawman* (2012), *West Texas Kill* (2012), *Return to Red River* (2017) and *Taos Lightning* (2019). He has also won the Western Heritage Wrangler Award from the National Cowboy and Western Heritage Museum for his novel *Spark on the Prairie: The Trial of the Kiowa Chiefs* (2004); the Arkansiana Award for Juvenile/Young Adult from the Arkansas Library Association for *Poison Spring* (2015); and the Milton F. Perry Award from the National James-Younger Gang for his novel *Northfield* (2007).

Boggs has also written for more than fifty newspapers and magazines, and is a frequent contributor to *Wild West* and *True West* magazines.

He lives with wife Lisa and son Jack in Santa Fe. His website is www.johnnydboggs.com.

Center Point Large Print
600 Brooks Road / PO Box 1
Thorndike, ME 04986-0001 USA

(207) 568-3717

US & Canada:
1 800 929-9108
www.centerpointlargeprint.com